AF424487

This story wasn't supposed to be a book.

It was born as a film script, scene by scene, frame by frame. It was written to be watched, not read. For a while, it was close to being made. But the weight of the film industry and the nature of what it dared to say, pushed it into silence.

I could've let it go. I didn't.

Instead, I chose to contain it on paper rather than on screen.

I won't call this a novel. It doesn't follow those rules. It's a story. A one-sitter read. Sharp. Tight. Visual. I wrote it in a way the reader could direct it the in their imagination, their mind's eye. Every page a cut. Every silence is intentional.

There's no fixed setting. No forced background. The names, the faces, the places - I leave for you decide. I've given just enough. The rest is yours. It doesn't follow the rules. But then again, neither do I.

I'm like Issac. I don't follow the rules

Chapter 1
Prologue

Beethoven's *Für Elise* drifted through the old chapel, threading gently into the crisp mountain air of Ooty's valley-a place tourists adored for its charm. But to a trained ear, the notes rang flawed. Issac's fingers hesitated, missing beats, distorting rhythm. What should've been a masterpiece became a fractured echo of genius, each wrong key exposing the weight in his hands.

But who would notice that in this near-forgotten, dusty chapel with its cracked pews and shadows older than memory-except Vicar Abraham Noah, now ninety and moving slower with a worn metal crutch, who sat quietly, watching Issac stumble through the masterpiece with something close to fatherly pride. The same quiet pride he reserved for all the children once abandoned, now housed in what Issac had insisted be renamed Noah's Children's Home. Not an orphanage. A home.

The battered piano had been Issac's only constant. His first friend. His first voice. It still sat in the same spot where Father Noah had found him-just a baby-wrapped in silence and swaddled in mystery, laid at the altar like an offering, forty - six years ago.

Unaware that Noah, now well into his nineties, had crept in behind him, Issac played on, fingers struggling to coax beauty from keys that had long gone mute and dust-clogged. He tapped the sostenuto pedal, coaxing it like a stubborn old mule.

"It's older than me, so go easy," came the voice - rough as gravel, but warm.

Issac turned, and before a word left his mouth, he was pulled into Noah's arms. The embrace hit him like a wave, collapsing the years between them. It wasn't just a greeting -it was forgiveness, memory, and belonging. For a moment, the pain he was carrying was shared, and not spoken.

The children called him Father Noah because of the collar, the calm, the scriptures and the sermons. But to Isaac, he was *Papa* the only one he ever knew. The only one soul he ever let in.

Noah's fondness for the boy had always been obvious. Isaac wasn't just the first to arrive - he was also the one with the insatiable mind. Every weekend, Noah brought him a new book. Issac devoured them like candy. By ten, he'd devoured the entire Hardy Boys series- not just for the thrill, but for the method. Each page taught him how to think like a detective, to chase truth with instinct sharpened by fiction.

Issac's bond with Father Noah had shaped more than his childhood. it had forged a foundation. In that quiet comfort, he blossomed. Music, sports, academics- whatever he touched, he mastered with a focus far beyond his years. But brilliance couldn't always fill the silence left by a mother's absence. On those days, Issac would vanish into the little library Noah had built for the children, losing himself in stories when real comfort was out of reach.

It came as no surprise to Father Noah when Issac topped the civil services exams. He didn't chase power - he chose purpose. The badge wasn't about power. It was a tool. The Indian Police Service gave him a way to fight for the voiceless.

On the day of the convocation, Issac had only one request - that Father Noah witness the passing-out parade. For the old priest, it was a bittersweet moment.

The man who preached of God's grace for the forgotten, now stood watching a child once abandoned, stand taller than the rest.

Days before Issac left to join as Assistant Commissioner, Crime Division, Chennai, Noah handed him his old Bible - leather-bound, softened by time and use. Inside, a yellowing card with fading ink bore a verse:

"Open your mouth for the mute, for the rights of all who are destitute. Speak up and judge fairly; defend the rights of the poor and needy." Proverbs 31:8–9

Issac read it every morning before he put on the badge.

It wasn't just scripture. It became a compass. Oath. A line first drawn, then etched into his soul - reminding him why he couldn't look away from the violated, the voiceless, or the crimes some "good men" chose to ignore.

"Have you heard from Ineya?"

Father Noah's question came softly, his fingers gently wrapping around Issac's. No accusation. Just worry, dressed as prayer.

Issac's silence said enough.

Noah nodded. "May God bless and protect her, wherever she may be."

Issac had asked him more than once to move in with him. Better care. Modern comforts. But Noah always refused, quoting Ecclesiastes: "There is a time to live, and a time to die."

That line haunted Issac. Made him feel ten again, on the verge of losing everything.

"I wish I died before you, Papa," he whispered. "I don't know what I'm doing anymore."

Noah's grip tightened. "My son," he said 'seldom-used' words, always followed by truth.

"Your purpose isn't about what you want. It's about what others need. God wrote your story even before you were born. It's not over. Not yet."

Issac looked down at their hands. One gnarled with age. One calloused by work. And for the first time in months, he felt steady.

Chapter 2
Issac and Ineya

"Have you heard from Ineya?"

Father Noah's voice lingered in Issac's ears as he drove through the winding highway back to Cochin - his current home and weekend refuge.

He had once served as the Commissioner of Police there, a role that devoured his time and sleep in equal measure. But now, stationed at the State Crime Records Bureau in Trivandrum, Issac had stepped into a quieter post. It wasn't easy, but it didn't consume him like before. The sleepless nights that had defined his years in the crime division were now behind him.

Issac had been a workaholic - driven by an addictive rush each time a new case hit his desk. The harder it was, the more alive he felt. He chased justice with obsession, honoring a silent promise made to Father Noah. But that same drive had come at a cost.

It was Ineya's main accusation: he never had time for her or for them. She had always felt like a footnote in a life ruled by duty.

He had another hour before he'd hit the highway - then four more until Cochin. If traffic stayed light, he might push the speed limit; out-of-state plates rarely got flagged. But what he needed now was music.

His playlist was a curated sanctuary: Chopin, Beethoven, and Bach composers who sharpened his mind and softened his thoughts. In another life, maybe he could've been one of them - composing symphonies instead of case reports. A man who healed through music, not justice.

As Rachmaninoff's "Concerto No. 2" poured through the car, Issac let the sound fill the silence Ineya had left behind.

"How can anyone not appreciate this?" he wondered. Then smirked to himself. Ineya, his ex-wife - for one.

"Have you heard from Ineya?" Issac knew he never would.

Despite how broken it all became, he had loved her -truly, deeply. But some things aren't built to last. They were opposites in every way: he found solace in Chopin; she blared heavy metal through the walls. A classical soul and a storm under one roof-it was bound to break.

Issac was tall and dark-not conventionally handsome, but quietly commanding. His presence came from precision, from a confidence that spoke with few words. Ineya, on the other hand, turned heads without trying-fair-skinned, deep brown eyes, beauty that entered a room before she did.

The one thing that tethered them was pain: both had grown up as orphans. Issac was raised in a children's home; Ineya, in a strict convent where affection was rationed and silence was sacred.

Ineya's mother had supported her financially from a distance, but their only meeting-during her college admission in Chennai-left a wound that never healed. That's when Ineya learned the truth: she was born from a one-night stand between her mother and a French tourist. Soon after, her mother married someone else and moved to England, closing the door behind her.

At eighteen, Ineya came into a sizable inheritance. But instead of freedom, it became a trap. She spiraled-substance abuse, reckless relationships, a need to numb what couldn't be undone.

This mix of wealth and independence turned toxic for Ineya, fueling a slow, volatile spiral. What should've been freedom became a trap she walked into willingly-numb, reckless, unafraid of consequence.

She burned through nights at flashy pubs and seedy clubs, stumbling out drunk or dazed, mascara smudged and memories missing. It wasn't about fun. It was about forgetting. The more she unraveled, the more invisible she became.

Predatory men waited in the margins. They didn't need to stalk-just linger. Her vulnerability made their job easy. She was too high to notice, too broken to fight.

The final blow came when she was expelled from college. The shame didn't crush her-it confirmed what she already feared: she was lost, unwanted, and spiraling fast.

That night, in a haze of liquor and smoke, Ineya lay still on her bed, staring at the ceiling fan spinning above her.

"Can it hold my weight?" she wondered, the thought landing like a whisper in her mind.

The bottle of rum beside her was nearly empty. Her body hummed with exhaustion. She lit another cigarette, letting the smoke dull her senses, and played her favorite song-"Paranoid" by Ozzy Osbourne.

The lyrics struck like confession:

"And so as you hear these words Telling you now of my state

I tell you to enjoy life

I wish I could, but it's too late."

The acrid smoke burned her lungs as she dragged deep, the cigarette trembling between her fingers. She played the song again, letting Ozzy's voice seep into her bones. There was something twisted and comforting in those words. The rum's bitter taste clung to her tongue, making her grimace.

"This cheap liquor is disgusting," she muttered, knowing full well she'd drink every last drop. If it dulled the ache, it was worth it.

Getting more alcohol in Chennai was never a problem. She had the peddler's number saved under a fake name. But tonight, he said he had no transport. And she just couldn't wait until morning.

Fueled by the music and a fresh wave of emptiness, she threw on her hoodie and track pants-still stained from god knows what-and stepped into the night.

The air slapped her awake. Cold. Cruel. Familiar.

She moved like muscle memory through the shortcuts that wound toward her college-the peddler lived nearby, near the tracks. The sound of an approaching train hummed in the distance like a slow, metallic warning.

"Once I'm drunk enough," she thought, "I'll hug a train and let it take care of the rest."

She paid the peddler extra for the rum, her eyes scanning the empty road as she vanished into the shadows.

Her destination: the college girl's secret spot. Tucked behind the college campus, hidden by overgrowth and apathy, it was where girls used to sneak off to smoke and gossip. Now it was hers alone.

The railway track stood just twenty paces away. Cold. Straight. Final.

She unscrewed the bottle and took a long, punishing swig.

"At least I should've gotten better booze for my last night," she muttered. And waited.

A murder case had lingered too long, casting a cloud of frustration over the city. When Issac took charge in Chennai, the cold file landed on his desk-and he made it personal. He wasn't one to leave shadows unchallenged.

Clue by clue, he dug in. Quiet. Relentless. He'd narrowed in on the culprits, but they were ghosts-always one step ahead, shifting hideouts and slipping through cracks in the system.

Issac didn't wait behind a desk. Night after night, he patrolled the city alone, his instincts sharp and Father Noah's quiet blessing in the back of his mind. He moved in disguise through bars, underground clubs, and back-alley dens-any place the desperate and dangerous called home.

One tip came from a trusted informant: the suspects might surface at the same peddler Ineya had visited earlier. It made sense. It was a dry day-bars and outlets were shuttered. If they needed booze, that peddler was the go-to.

Issac decided to watch the place himself.

To stay off the radar, he chose the rail track route-a narrow, grim corridor that curved dangerously close to the peddler's house... and even closer to where Ineya was. He split his team, posted them at key vantage points, and took the track himself. His boots crunched over gravel as his eyes swept the dark.

Caution in his breath. Anticipation in his blood. "I tell you... to enjoy life...

I wish I could... but it's too late..."

The silence shattered as Ineya's slurred singing echoed through the dark. Issac's jaw tightened. This was his only chance to corner the murderers, and now-this?

His first instinct was irritation. But something about the voice pulled at him. A woman's voice, alone, at this hour, near the tracks? He crept closer, scanning the shadows, body low, senses alert.

No use telling her to be quiet-she was clearly drunk, if not completely out of it. Just then, the distant horn of a train pierced the night. The girl stirred, trying to rise, stumbling as she clutched a half-empty bottle. She was seconds from stepping onto the tracks.

Issac moved fast.

He grabbed her from behind, his arm locking around her waist, the other hand gently muffling her mouth. She collapsed into him without resistance, her body limp, and head lolling onto his shoulder. She didn't flinch. Didn't scream. Just melted into him like it had happened before-a scene from too many forgotten nights.

The train thundered past, casting slices of light across the two of them. In the flickers of the train compartment lights, Issac caught a glimpse of her face. Messy curls and smudged makeup. But under it-striking beauty.

He brushed a strand of hair from her cheek. She blinked, opened her eyes for a second, and smiled faintly before letting the eyes close again.

Despite the stench of cheap liquor and the ragged clothes, something didn't fit. She didn't belong here. Not in that way.

"Spoiled rich kid?" Issac guessed.

But there was something else-an ache that lingered beneath the surface.

His mind raced.

"Who is she? What is she doing here? And why does she look like she's done this before?"

"Sir, we've got them!"

Issac's thoughts snapped back to reality as his team's triumphant voice cut through the night. The culprits had been apprehended-along with the peddler. But as they approached, their eyes flicked to the girl slumped in Issac's arms, puzzled.

Issac noticed the looks.

"I don't know her," he said, cutting off any assumptions. "She was drunk, making a ruckus. We'll take her in and get her ID."

She stirred as he spoke, still leaning into him, eyes fluttering open now and then. No panic. No awareness. Just a slow drift between sleep and stupor.

They began heading toward the old Willys jeep. The suspects were being loaded into the back when Ineya suddenly blinked, recognized the peddler-and snapped.

With a burst of drunken clarity, she slapped him hard across the face.

"Don't sell cheap alcohol, b****!" she slurred.

The tension cracked. Laughter broke through the fatigue. Even Issac's lips twitched at the corners.

Back at the station, after logging the arrests, one mystery remained: the girl. No missing person reports matched her description. The wireless channels across city stations came back empty.

She was temporarily placed in the second holding cell-a quieter one, with a small bed laid out on the floor. She didn't fight. She didn't speak. Just curled up and slept, her face peaceful, as if finally away from the noise in her head.

The team, hardened as they were, had already softened toward her. That slap. That strange charm.

And Issac-though trained to detach-couldn't help but feel it too.

Compassion, sure. But something else. Curiosity.

As Ineya began to sober up, Issac pieced together fragments of her story-and was struck by how much it echoed his own. Abandonment. Struggle. Silence. The resemblance stirred something in him. Compassion, yes. But deeper than that-recognition.

He called Father Noah.

Within a day, arrangements were made. Ineya was admitted to a quiet rehabilitation center under Father Noah's care. It marked the first real turning point in her life.

Issac started visiting her regularly. At first, their conversations were clipped-she hid behind sarcasm, and he behind silence. But slowly, the gap between them narrowed. She began to open up, revealing the chaos beneath her bravado. Issac, always more listener than speaker, let her unravel without interruption.

She mistook his quiet for depth. For wisdom. But in that silence, she felt seen-truly seen-for the first time in years.

He, in turn, was drawn to her resilience. Her raw honesty. And the way pain lived just behind her eyes.

Father Noah noticed the growing closeness and, with his usual soft encouragement, nudged them toward the idea of a future. Two broken souls, he believed, could still make something whole.

When Ineya completed her rehab program, she and Issac began spending time together outside the center. Long walks. Quiet meals. Shared silences.

Issac fell hard.

But Ineya's admiration wasn't just for the man.

It was for the position he held-the authority, the recognition, the way people paused when they heard his name. His recent assignment against the mafia had turned him into a public figure, a symbol of strength.

And that... that was what really pulled her in.

Despite their differences, they decided to take a chance on each other. With Father Noah's blessing, they tied the knot in a quiet ceremony at the chapel beside Noah's Children's Home-just the priest, a handful of helpers, and a few children from the orphanage.

As they exchanged vows, their promises were simple: to care, to support, and to try. Both knew the road ahead wouldn't be easy-but for that moment, they chose to believe in it.

But love, as the experts say, comes with a countdown.

Romance has a shelf life of twenty-two months-after which it demands effort, patience, and compromise. The spark gives way to routine, and routine gives way to cracks.

For Issac and Ineya, the first crack came in the shape of duty.

Issac was promoted to Commissioner of Police in Cochin-a small but bustling city in Kerala. The post was prestigious but punishing. Cochin's law and order system was tangled in politics, and many high-profile cases remained frozen in red tape.

Issac had been sent to change that.

And slowly, the man who once sat quietly beside Ineya at rehab dinners was now working twelve-hour days, taking calls through meals, and disappearing into silence she couldn't reach.

With near-unchecked freedom to operate, Issac thrived in his role. He cracked cases with surgical precision, outsmarted culprits, and earned admiration from both peers and superiors. But success came at a steep cost.

His time with Ineya began to vanish-minutes shaved away by late nights, early mornings, and an endless stream of high-stakes calls. Some days, she was asleep before he got home. Other days, she pretended to be.

Unbeknownst to Issac, Ineya's old demons had started to stir. The silence, the solitude, the fading attention-it pushed her back toward the edge. And slowly, she slipped into the grip of alcohol once again.

Despite the chaos, Issac always carved out time to speak with Father Noah. Curiously, so did Ineya. She often confided in the priest-about her loneliness, her frustrations, and her resentment toward her increasingly absent husband.

Father Noah, patient as ever, listened without judgment. And in gentle, hopeful tones, he encouraged both of them-separately-to start thinking about a child.

Issac, exhausted and distracted, misread it as a message from Ineya. A subtle request passed through Noah. He didn't realize she wasn't ready for motherhood-didn't want the weight of it just yet.

And truthfully, they weren't ready.

A baby required presence, patience, intimacy. Their life allowed none of it.

His schedule was erratic.

Her drinking-a secret Issac kept even from Father Noah-was getting worse.

Every time Issac or Ineya spoke with Father Noah, he would gently urge them to visit. He often reminded them he was getting old, dropping phrases like, "I may not be around much longer," with a soft smile that didn't quite hide the truth.

Lately, his conversations had taken a more pointed tone-dropping hints that Issac should meet "someone important" on his next visit. Issac sensed a quiet urgency in the old man's voice during their last call. On impulse, he requested a week's leave from work. It was approved without hesitation.

Ineya seemed pleased about the trip-or at least acted like it. Restless and emotionally adrift, she welcomed the idea of revisiting the one place that had once brought her peace. A visit to Father Noah was long overdue.

It was the priest's birthday, and they decided to make it special. They brought gifts, knowing full well that what he wanted most was their time.

The drive took just under seven hours, offering the perfect stretch for conversation. But instead of talking, they fell into silence-Issac handling official calls, Ineya texting friends, each wearing headphones, each in their own world.

Their lives had drifted.

Issac's circle was composed of officers, bureaucrats, and informants. Ineya's friends were strangers to him-young, fast, untethered. Even Issac's own colleagues barely knew her beyond a name and a few polite smiles at formal dinners.

Father Noah was overwhelmed with emotion as Issac and Ineya stepped through the doorway.

"Happy birthday, Papa!" they said in unison, wrapping him in a warm embrace.

The hug lasted long-long enough to show how much they had missed each other.

Father Noah's eyes welled up as he struggled to compose himself.

"God is good," he whispered. "He answers prayers. You know how long I've been asking Him for this moment."

Chapter 3
Issac, Ineya, and Aaliya

The heartfelt hug was gently broken by the sound of a violin-someone playing "Für Elise," but stumbling through the notes, struggling with rhythm and pitch. Issac's ears perked up. Who was playing?

He glanced at Father Noah, puzzled. The old man had told him he lived alone now, with only a caretaker for company. Church services had long ceased as newer denominations took over. The tune, though recognizable, was awkward-notes hit but offbeat, tentative, unsure.

Father Noah caught Issac's expression and smiled.

"One of the strings is broken," he said. "She's trying to find the notes on the others. And… her fingers are tiny."

"Who is she?" Issac and Ineya asked at once, curiosity now fully lit.

"That's Aaliya," Father Noah replied, his voice softening with affection. "The day after your wedding, I found her on the street-unconscious, clutching an old ektara. I couldn't leave her there. I brought her here."

He paused, pride glinting in his eyes.

"She's a prodigy, Issac. In just two years, she's mastered the piano-and now she's teaching herself the violin. Nobody trains her. She just listens once… and plays."

Issac's curiosity got the better of him. "Where is she from? Didn't anyone come looking for her?"

Father Noah's expression darkened as he gestured for them to follow. From the next room, the fractured melody of the broken violin continued.

"I suspect she was part of a gypsy gang," he said quietly. "They might've abandoned her. Or left her to die. She was gravely ill when I found her."

Issac pressed on, his police mind already spinning with questions. "Did you ask her anything about her past? What language does she speak?"

Father Noah's reply was gentle, almost reverent. "Sign language."

Issac and Ineya exchanged a surprised glance.

"She's mute," Father Noah added, compassion in his voice. "But that's the only challenge God placed on her. He blessed her with the rest. When I found her, she looked no older than six. It's been two years now-and her growth, her gift… it humbles me every day."

Issac's mind instinctively drew parallels to the street children he had encountered-faces too young for the horrors they'd seen. He had seen the blank stares behind glassy eyes, their innocence twisted by exploitation. Many were trafficked, forced into begging or petty sales, often mutilated to evoke pity. The memory of those children haunted him, igniting a fire within to be a voice for the voiceless.

But Aaliya defied every image he had imagined.

Instead of a frail, broken child, a curly-haired girl with striking blue eyes sat quietly by the window sill, the morning sun casting a golden halo around her. Her rosy cheeks, button nose, and delicate features radiated innocence and quiet strength-beauty untouched by her turbulent past.

Both Issac and Ineya were momentarily taken aback. Ineya couldn't help but notice the resemblance-the wild curls, the small frame. Aaliya looked like a

Miniature version of herself. But for Issac, the reaction was deeper. Something paternal stirred in him-a wave of unexpected emotion, a silent pull toward the girl who now played broken notes on a weathered violin.

As soon as she saw them, Aaliya left her violin and rushed toward them. She politely greeted Issac and Ineya, then gave them each a warm hug. She tried to say something, her hands fluttering with eagerness, but Issac and Ineya exchanged helpless looks-they couldn't understand her.

Father Noah stepped in. "She's saying she's been waiting for both of you. I talk about you often, and she's excited to finally meet you."

A flurry of sign language followed. Only Father Noah could follow the rapid gestures, and once she was done, he translated, "She says she wanted to have breakfast with you. She specially asked the caretaker to get idli and sambar because she heard its Ineya's favorite. And by the way, Ineya, she thinks you're very pretty."

Issac grinned. "So, you don't like me?"

Aaliya shot back a quick response in sign language, and Father Noah chuckled as he interpreted, "She said she's been waiting to hear you play the piano."

The next couple of days were a whirlwind of excitement for all of them. Ineya cherished her time with Father Noah. He often shared his biblical wisdom with both her and Issac about the importance of having a family. However, Ineya wasn't ready to bear a child. Her concerns stemmed from a fear that pregnancy might alter her physical appearance, or perhaps it was the lingering trauma from her childhood. She doubted her ability to fit into the role of a mother, and Father Noah's words of wisdom couldn't convince her otherwise.

Aaliya, on the other hand, was overjoyed with the electric violin Issac gifted her the day after they met. The evening piano sessions with Issac became a delightful entertainment for everyone. It took Issac only a couple of days to grasp the basics of sign language, while Ineya picked up a little, though she didn't put in much effort. Instead, she often took solitary evening walks, leaving Issac to spend quality time with Father Noah and Aaliya.

The bond between Aaliya and Issac grew extremely strong. Aaliya thrived under Issac's musical guidance, and he was thrilled to see her quickly grasp lessons on both the piano and violin. He couldn't help but wonder if Aaliya was an alter ego of himself. What drew him to her was her remarkable discipline and dedication. Every morning, she would wake up early, complete her Bible reading and prayers, and tackle her academics with diligence. Despite being homeschooled, Aaliya not only kept pace with her syllabus but also surpassed expectations for an eight-year-old, demonstrating a thirst for knowledge that impressed Issac.

"Can I come with you?" Issac asked, breaking the silence as Ineya slipped on her walking shoes. The question caught her off guard-he had never once asked to join her on these walks, her only remaining ritual of solitude.

She turned to him, surprised, but didn't say no. Part of her wanted to believe it was a sweet gesture, a sign that their time here was softening something in him. But another part-the part that had learned to trust her gut-felt a subtle shift.

Women have a sixth sense for these things, an emotional radar tuned to the smallest deviations in tone, timing, or touch. And right now, that radar was quietly pinging. Something was off. Issac never did anything without reason, and this sudden need to accompany her didn't come from nowhere.

Issac's firm grip on Ineya's hands startled her-a gesture she hadn't felt since their courting days. The silence between them was thick, broken only by the distant chatter of birds. Ineya's mind raced. What had stirred this sudden show of tenderness?

They stood at her favorite overlook, where the sun dipped behind the Western Ghats, painting the sky in hues of molten gold and blood-orange. She glanced at Issac, wondering if he, raised in this very place, still felt moved by the view-or had it become just another backdrop to his routines ?

She had always fantasized about a life in Delhi-its energy, its ambition-and she had mentioned it more than once. Even Father Noah had gently lobbied on her behalf, planting the seed in Issac's mind. Maybe this quiet moment, bathed in warmth and soft light, was her best chance. One final push to make her dream real. To trade silence for conversation. To make plans.

"Can we take Aaliya home?" Issac's question landed like a stone in still water. Ineya froze, caught off guard. When she met his eyes, she saw something unexpected-hope, warmth, and a father's quiet yearning.

Her mind spiraled. Aaliya could be the spark their fading bond needed. A living, breathing distraction from the silence between them. Better yet, with Aaliya around, no one would press her about getting pregnant-at least not for a while. And maybe, just maybe, this was her chance to finally nudge Issac toward Delhi. She could frame it as a fresh start-for Aaliya's future and of course for all of them.

The evening before their departure, Aaliya's absence from the usual music session raised quiet alarm. Issac, Ineya, and Father Noah split up, searching her room and nearby corners.

"She'll be at the church," Father Noah said softly, already knowing. "It's where she goes when she's overwhelmed. Joy or sorrow-it always leads her there."

Inside the dim church, they found her on a pew, head bowed, and tears streaking her face as her fingers moved in silent communion with God. Issac and Ineya joined her on either side-one family, briefly unbroken. She leaned into Issac, gripping Ineya's hand, her sign language slow but clear: *"I'll miss you both. I'll pray for you every day."*

Aaliya glanced at Father Noah. He smiled through the mist in his eyes, saying nothing. No one needed words anymore.

"Come, let's go pack," Issac said gently, resting a hand on her shoulder.

Aaliya signed back with a small plea: *"Let me stay here a little longer. You go finish packing. I'll meet you at the dinner table."*

Issac and Ineya exchanged a look-bittersweet, bracing.

"We've packed already, Aaliya," Issac said quietly. "We meant your things."

Eight-year-old minds take time to process unexpected adult decisions. Aaliya's quizzical gaze darted between Ineya and Issac, her eyes silently inquired, "What meaneth this?"

Issac's gentle smile softened her confusion. "You're coming with us," he said quietly. "Now, can we go pack your things?"

Aaliya's face lit up. Without another sign, she jumped off the pew and threw her arms around Issac, holding him tight, wordless in her joy. They say a child is born from a mother's womb - but in this case a child was born from the heart of a father. And in that moment, something quietly shifted. She wasn't just leaving with them. She was already his.

Chapter 4

The day the music died.

"Have you heard from Ineya?"

Father Noah's voice echoed in Issac's mind as he pulled into the driveway of his Cochin home-*Aaliya*, named after the child who filled his world with meaning. The house, once a symbol of his union with Ineya, had quietly transformed into a shrine of fatherly devotion.

But life had shifted. What once felt like love's steady course had begun to fray at the edges. In the early days, Ineya had confided in Father Noah about Issac's long absences. Now, her frustrations had taken a sharper turn-she felt sidelined, no longer competing with Issac's work, but with a child. Aaliya had become the center of his universe, and Ineya, increasingly, a distant satellite. Her sense of abandonment was no longer subtle-it was raw, growing with every affectionate glance Issac spared for the little girl and not her.

Issac, oblivious to the growing void, threw himself deeper into his work and into caring for Aaliya, finding unexpected peace in their blossoming bond. Meanwhile, Ineya clung to her independence, carving out a work-from-home role with a Delhi-based corporate firm. Her biweekly trips to the capital-"a necessity for the job," she insisted-further strained the already fragile fabric of their marriage. The thread that once held them together, delicate to begin with, had begun to quietly unravel.

The day Issac was promoted to Commissioner of Police, Crime Branch, Cochin City-what should have been a triumphant milestone-was shattered by a single, devastating phone call. As colleagues gathered to celebrate, a call from Aaliya's school brought him to his knees: Aaliya had fallen from the balcony of the school building.

She was no more.

The words slammed into him like a freight train.

His breath caught, the room spun, and for a moment, everything else-the promotion, the people, the noise-faded into silence. Aaliyah... No more.

The once-vibrant school campus, filled with the sounds of laughter and learning, had turned into a scene of unspeakable tragedy. The sixth floor, where she had spent countless joyful hours practicing music and attending cultural events, had now become the site of unbearable loss.

And Issac-his world crumbled around him. Consumed by grief, he turned to alcohol for solace, but it only accelerated his downward spiral.

Ineya, who had been emotionally distant for a while, finally severed ties and relocated to Delhi permanently. Father Noah tried reaching out to her, but she had seemingly vanished. Her old number was disconnected-predictably-and all attempts at communication were met with an unsettling silence.

Issac applied for voluntary retirement, but Amardeep Singh-the Director General of Police and his mentor-declined to accept it. Instead, Amardeep granted Issac a two-month leave, hoping the break would help him heal.

But the leave only deepened Issac's despair. Alcohol became his crutch, pulling him further into a void he couldn't climb out of.

When he returned, he once again requested voluntary retirement. For the second time, Amardeep refused-citing Issac's unmatched contribution to the force. Though Issac's successes were often overshadowed by seniors and politician's hungry for credit, he never cared for applause; his rush came from cracking the case.

Recognizing that his talents were still needed, Amardeep reassigned him to the State Crime Records Bureau (SCRB), hoping a shift in environment would help. Out of respect and loyalty to his mentor, Issac didn't resist.

Chapter 5
Even in sleep

The car came to a halt outside his house in Cochin - a house that once echoed with laughter, now heavy with silence. The drive home had stirred more than just memories; it had reopened wounds he thought he'd buried. Aaliya would have been fifteen by now, he thought, the ache still fresh.

The house, now a shrine to Aaliya's memory, remained untouched by time. Issac often wandered into her room, half-expecting to see her bright smile or hear the echo of her laughter.

A large photo of Aaliya dominated the main hall, recreating the imagery of Issac's first meeting with her at Father Noah's children's home. After her passing, he had moved the picture from her bedroom to the living room, placing it above her silent violin case.

The only addition to the house since his separation from Ineya and Aaliya was the breakfast nook he'd built with his own hands. On its ledge sat an open Bible, bookmarked at his favorite verse from Proverbs 31. From this quiet corner, Issac began each morning - either sipping coffee or, more often, chasing away hangovers with a bitter gulp of the "morning after" drink. And always, his eyes would drift to Aaliya's picture.

Tomorrow morning wouldn't bring any reprieve. The solo drive back from Father Noah's had drained him, and the flood of memories only amplified his craving for alcohol. He had hit rock bottom, relying on a toxic cocktail of melatonin and whiskey to catch fragments of sleep. But even that offered no escape-his dreams were haunted by demons that taunted him with cruel clarity.

In search of fleeting peace, Issac downed two quick shots of whiskey, then tossed a couple of chicken pieces into the microwave before stepping into the shower.

Later, he poured himself another shot, the burn tracing down his throat like a punishment he welcomed. The chicken sat untouched; alcohol was easier to swallow. He'd lost track of how many drinks he'd had-or even what time it was. As the room began to spin, a familiar numbness settled over him, dulling everything.

Pushing off from the couch, Issac staggered to his bedroom. He collapsed onto the bed, the sheets rising around him like fog. Just before sleep took over, he felt the whiskey glass slip from his fingers and heard it shatter on the floor.

But even in sleep, Issac couldn't outrun his demons. His dreams conjured Aaliya, standing alone in a vast, lush green field, dressed in black, her cello cradled in her arms. Her tiny fingers moved with urgency, but they were bleeding-scarlet streaks trickling down the strings and pooling at the base of the instrument.

From the edges of the dreamscape, dark figures began to emerge-faceless, cloaked in black, gliding silently toward her. Aaliya's curls bounced as she turned to run, her silent pleas echoing in Issac's ears, though her lips never moved. The shadows gained ground, closing in fast.

She reached the edge of a cliff, panic in her eyes, with no way out. As the faceless figures loomed, Aaliya looked back one last time, then stepped into the void-disappearing into the darkness below.

Chapter 6
Wake up call

The sharp buzz of his phone sliced through Issac's sleep, dragging him out of yet another nightmare. He fumbled for the device, his vision still foggy. Four missed calls. All from DGP Amardeep Singh.

"What the hell?" Issac muttered, blinking at the screen. The time glared back at him: 4:44 AM. His alarm hadn't gone off in days, and now this.

Whatever it was, it had to be serious.

He hit redial, the chill of the hour settling into his spine as he waited.

"Issac, have you reached Trivandrum?" came Amardeep Singh's voice, cool and to the point.

No apology. No greeting. Just straight to business.

Issac rubbed his face, exhaling. Waking someone up before sunrise should be a criminal offense, he thought.

"Sir, I... reached... last night... Cochin..." Issac stammered, still shaking off the fog of sleep.

The DGP cut him off sharply. "I want you to leave Cochin immediately. How long will it take you to reach Trivandrum?"

"About three hours, sir," Issac replied, sitting up straighter.

"Good. Be at my office by eleven. You've got enough time."

"Yes, sir," Issac said, but his mind was already racing. What could be so urgent? Why now? And why him?

Chapter 7
The first body

"Good morning, and here are the headlines for today," the news anchor announced, her upbeat tone slicing through the silence as Issac forced down a sip of his morning coffee and a bite of toast. He had long stopped trusting those chirpy greetings-they usually preceded a flood of bad news. Good news, after all, had become a rare species.

Lawlessness had surged since Issac stepped away from the Crime Department-a brutal reminder that when good men retreat, evil doesn't hesitate to take their place.

During his tenure, Issac had kept the city's underbelly in check with an iron will and sleepless nights. One of his most effective contributions had been the proposal to install CCTV cameras in high-crime zones across major cities. He had pushed the plan through the DGP and government channels, assembling a young, razor-sharp team to monitor the feeds and preempt criminal activity. The results had spoken for themselves.

But after his departure, the gears began to grind slower. Without Issac's drive to lead them, the team lost steam-and slowly, so did the system.

This morning was no different-except it had captured headlines across every major network. The reason? It involved Mr. Williams, a senior figure in the ruling party and a man well-known for his ruthless grip on power.

Williams had a long, murky trail of scandals and whispered allegations behind him-shady business deals, political arm-twisting, and a talent for making enemies. His brash demeanor and unapologetic tongue had landed him in hot water more times than the media could count.

He owned-or rather, his wife officially did-a sprawling 27,000-square-foot property in the heart of Trivandrum. The estate had been locked in a vicious civil dispute for over five years, but as always, Williams' influence tipped the scales. Just a month ago, the verdict fell conveniently in his favor.

Wasting no time, he flipped the property to a local developer. Excavation work began almost immediately.

But as the machines tore into the earth, the crew stumbled upon something grim-human remains, a skeleton buried beneath the soil.

The police were promptly alerted, and a team led by Alex-a sharp and astute Circle Inspector-was dispatched to the scene. The opposition party pounced on the opportunity, wasting no time in pointing fingers. They accused Mr. Williams of being directly linked to the buried skeleton, citing his chequered past as evidence. Demands for a swift investigation escalated, with calls for the ruling party's resignation gaining momentum. As the story spread like wildfire, Mr. Williams' refusal to comment only intensified the media frenzy and fanned the flames of political outrage.

Upon arriving at the scene, Circle Inspector Alex noted that the police had managed to control the crowd and keep the media at a distance. Still, the muffled chatter of reporters lingered in the air-speculative, exaggerated, and irresponsibly confident. To them, the truth was secondary to breaking news and viewer ratings.

"I'm sick and tired of these useless idiots," Alex muttered, the irritation clear in his voice. "Keep them back. Don't let them anywhere near the scene," he instructed a junior officer who had approached with a salute.

Snapping on a pair of gloves retrieved from the nearby ambulance, Alex turned to his subordinate, who had been surveying the site. "What's your initial take?"

"The body's severely decomposed, sir," the officer replied. "Can't make out any clear features."

Alex sighed, his gaze sweeping the area with the efficiency of a seasoned investigator. "Mr. Williams never ceases to get into trouble," he murmured to himself as he moved closer to the dig site, eyes alert for any missed detail.

Alex crouched near the remains, his eyes scanning every detail. He studied the pelvic structure, the long strands of matted hair, and the scraps of decayed fabric still clinging to the bones.

"It's female," he said flatly, no room for doubt.

His gaze shifted to the upper portion of the skull. Something was off. The back of the cranium was partially missing.

"Look at this," he said, gesturing to the damage. "The skull's fractured here. Did you find any bone fragments nearby?"

The subordinate shook his head. "We noticed that too, sir. Searched the area top to bottom-nothing turned up."

Alex's expression tightened, eyes narrowing. "Damn. This case's going to be one hell of a thing to crack."

Alex's phone buzzed in his pocket. He glanced at the screen-DGP Amardeep Singh.

"Alex, any leads yet?" the DGP asked without preamble. "Sir, I'm still going over the scene," Alex replied. "But there's something I need to discuss-better not over the phone. Can I meet you at your office?"

"Negative," Amardeep said. "The Chief Minister's summoned me and ADGP Khanna to the guest house. If it's confidential, meet us there."

"Understood, sir," Alex said, ending the call.

He turned back to his team. "Send the body to the forensic lab. I want an age estimate ASAP. Once that's in, cross-check it against all missing persons reports from that timeframe."

His eyes swept the site one last time, jaw clenched. "And keep the media out of this. Not a word leaks-understood?"

Chapter 8

One of five

Alex stepped out of his car and stood on the driveway of the minister's guest house. Just as he lit a cigarette, a white SUV rolled in. Spotting the DGP and ADGP, he quickly flicked the cigarette away, straightened his posture, and approached with a sharp salute.

"Sir, preliminary signs point to homicide," Alex began, his voice firm and professional. "From what I observed at the scene, the skeletal remains seem to be around two years old. But I'd rather reserve that call until forensics confirms."

DGP Amardeep Singh nodded thoughtfully. "Understood. We'll let the lab speak first."

Alex hesitated a beat, then continued, "Sir, there's one more detail-possibly relevant-but I'd prefer to discuss it in private. With your permission."

"Go on," the DGP said, more intrigued than alarmed.

"We've had four unsolved homicides in Cochin over the last four years," Alex said steadily. "This find in Trivandrum could be the fifth. The similarities are too sharp to ignore. I believe we might be looking at a connected pattern."

ADGP Khanna's eyes narrowed. "Are you suggesting-"

"Yes, sir," Alex cut in, firm. "It's possible we're dealing with a serial killer." A beat of silence followed. The weight of the revelation settled between them, heavy and undeniable.

DGP Singh gave a slow nod, his face unreadable. Khanna exchanged a glance with him, then turned to Alex. "Alright. Gather everything you've got and meet us at the office," he said. "We'll regroup there."

Chapter 9
Bring Issac in

The Chief Minister burst into the meeting room, his face creased with deep worry lines. "Williams denies any involvement in the murder," he briefed DGP Amardeep Singh and ADGP Khanna, his voice tinged with concern. But that wasn't his main worry. "Tomorrow's cabinet meeting," he continued, "the opposition will demand my resignation." He paused, his eyes scanning theirs, desperate for reassurance. "Do you have any leads yet?"

DGP Singh nodded with measured calm. "We're working on it, sir. Identifying the body will take at least two days."

The Minister's expression darkened. "Two days is too long. I need something to counter them tomorrow."

Singh leaned forward, lowering his voice. "Sir, we believe this murder may be connected to a serial killer. The pattern is too distinct to ignore."

The Minister's face lit up with a flicker of hope. "Serial killer? You're sure about that?"

DGP Singh gave a firm nod. "Over the years, we've discovered four bodies bearing similar injuries-most notably, crushed skulls. This morning's victim follows the same pattern. The consistency strongly suggests a serial offender, sir."

The Minister's eyes gleamed, a calculating glint cutting through his anxiety. He took a deep breath. "This could be my lifeline," he muttered. "If we go public with the serial killer theory, it could shift the spotlight away from Williams and my administration."

"Sir," Singh interjected, his tone steady but insistent, "this can't just be a political smokescreen. Our investigation genuinely points toward a serial killer. The evidence spans four cases from different stations in Cochin-and now, one in Trivandrum. I strongly recommend we consolidate these cases under a single task force. It's the only way we'll be able to see the full picture."

"What do you have in mind?" the Chief Minister asked, his tone laced with urgency.

"We need to bring Issac in on this case," ADGP Khanna suggested, his voice steady with conviction.

"I concur," DGP Singh added with a nod. "If we want swift and solid results, he's our best bet."

The Minister's brow furrowed. "But isn't he… unstable?" he asked cautiously. "I was told he left the Crime Branch on his own."

"He did," Khanna acknowledged, "but he's doing better now. We can reinstate him-temporarily, at least. He's still one of the finest investigators we've ever had."

The Minister's gaze sharpened. "Tell me more."

Khanna continued, "He has unmatched instincts in homicide cases. If this is a serial killer, we need someone who can think like one. And Issac can."

The Minister paused, clearly weighing the risks. "Are you both absolutely sure? I need results before the cabinet session ends. No room for error."

"We're certain, sir," Singh and Khanna said in unison, their expressions firm.

The Minister gave a decisive nod. "Then go for it."

Chapter 10
Dragged in

As Issac reported to the DGP's office, he braced himself for the usual pleasantries and questions about his well-being. But today, DGP Singh's demeanor was different-grim, focused, and devoid of formalities.

"We have a situation, Issac," Singh said, gesturing for him to sit. His voice was firm, his eyes sharp. "We believe there's a serial killer on the loose."

He picked up the remote and switched off the television, which was still buzzing with news coverage. "I assume you've seen the headlines."

"Caught a bit of it on the morning broadcast," Issac replied, already sensing the gravity of what was coming.

Singh leaned forward, lowering his voice. "This case is a powder keg. The Chief Minister's worried it could cost him the government. Media's circling like vultures. We need someone who can cut through the noise and deliver results. You're our best bet."

He paused, letting the weight of the assignment settle in. "Effective immediately, this is your case."

The weight in DGP Singh's voice was unmistakable. "Sir, please-" Issac began, but the DGP cut him off.

"It's a direct order from the Chief Minister," he said, handing Issac an envelope with the official seal. "You're taking this case, Issac. Circle Inspector Alex is waiting for you in the conference hall. He'll brief you and report back to me. You may leave now."

His tone was final.

Issac's heart sank. This case would demand every last shred of focus and fire he had left-except there was nothing left to give. The spark that once drove him had long since died.

As he stood and saluted his mentor, a thought flashed through his mind: *Let this be the second-to-last salute.*

"I'm going to resign," he told himself as he walked toward the conference hall, his mind scrambling for an escape from the case he'd just been chained to.

Chapter 11
Method of madness

Circle Inspector Alex stood in the corridor, puffing on a cigarette. The moment he saw Issac approaching the conference room, he quickly stubbed it out and straightened up. He greeted him with a salute.

"Cigarettes are going to kill you one day," Issac said dryly, returning the salute.

"Sir, it's my only stress buster," Alex replied with a faint, respectful smile as he opened the door to the conference hall.

As they stepped inside, Alex's energy shifted-eager, focused. "Sir, I've heard a lot about you. Always hoped I'd get a chance to work under your command. I believe the details I've compiled on this case will give us a solid place to begin."

Issac was quietly impressed by Alex's eagerness. The young officer radiated initiative and focus. His laptop was already connected to the TV, the screen aglow-proof of a no-nonsense attitude and a hunger to get moving.

"Sir, I've identified a few unsolved murders from the past," Alex began, standing beside the screen. "Before I walk you through the specifics, I'd like you to note the pattern. In each case, the skull was severely damaged." He paused, locking eyes with Issac. "The only difference between those and this morning's discovery is the location. All four took place in Cochin. This one's 260 kilometers away. Which means-we might just be scratching the surface."

As Alex dove into his presentation, Issac's initial detachment shifted. The mention of Cochin stirred something in him. His mind flashed to *Aaliya*-the house he'd built for his daughter, now a shrine to a memory that refused to fade. The thought of returning there, of being close to where Aaliya's presence still lingered, sent a flicker of emotion through his weary core. For the first time in a long while, the burden of the case felt almost-bearable.

Issac's gaze locked onto the screen as Alex's presentation took a darker turn. The images that followed hit harder than expected-side-by-side shots of victims in life and in death. Smiling faces frozen in time, followed by the brutality that ended them.

Issac leaned forward slightly, his eyes narrowing as he studied each frame. He wasn't just looking for evidence-he was hunting for a thread, a crack in the chaos, something that might give shape to the monster behind it all. The room fell silent but for the low hum of the projector.

"Victim #1: Sandra, originally from Alappuzha. Thirty-one years old at the time of her death," Alex narrated, his tone measured. "She was an assistant manager at Nexa Bank. Her remains were discovered in the 'Holy World' apartment complex near South Junction, Cochin."

Issac's eyes narrowed as he absorbed the details.

"The building had been under a long-standing legal dispute in the High Court," Alex added. "It was completely vacant when the murder occurred."

The image on the screen zoomed in to show Sandra's skull, the screen's harsh glow emphasizing the grotesque void where bone should have been.

"Note the damage, sir." Alex pointed to the display. "The skull was shattered. Fragments were missing-just like the others. This pattern repeats across the next three cases."

The brutality of it wasn't random. It was deliberate. Calculated. And that repetition was starting to tell its own story-one that hinted at something far more chilling than coincidence.

"Victim #2: Ashok, thirty-five. A restaurant owner from Thrissur," Alex continued. "He had a history of financial fraud-small-time scams, bounced cheques, unpaid debts. Initially, the case pointed toward local goons or loan sharks, but no connection could be proven. Eventually, the investigation hit a wall."

He clicked to the next image. It showed a dilapidated building.

"His body was found here," Alex said, his tone colder now. "Another abandoned property-this one empty for over six years."

The screen zoomed in on Ashok's skull. Like Sandra's, it was fractured and incomplete. The bone was split in near-identical fashion.

Issac leaned forward, studying the screen. The pattern was no longer a coincidence. It was beginning to look like a calling card.

"Victim #3: Hafsana. Twenty-eight. A prominent entrepreneur from Calicut," Alex said, tapping the keyboard. "She ran a high-end bridal makeup boutique in Cochin-well-known, well-liked."

Issac glanced at the screen as Hafsana's smiling portrait filled it. The next slide cut to the crime scene.

"Her husband was our initial suspect-he works in Dubai-but his alibi held. We had nothing on him. Her body was discovered in an abandoned ice factory just outside the city. The place was shut down then, but it's operational now."

Alex's tone hardened as he clicked to the forensic photos.

"This one's recent-only six months ago. Same skull trauma. Same setting. Different locations."

"Victim #4: Alfred, age thirty-four, originally from Quilon," Alex continued, clicking to the next slide. "A respected private tutor who ran his own coaching institute. Divorced, but widely admired in his community-especially by his students."

Issac stared at the screen as Alfred's profile faded into a forensic image. The next photo showed the derelict shell of the abandoned structure where the body had been found.

"His remains turned up in an abandoned building," Alex said, pausing to let the weight of that settle. "That's another link in this chain."

He straightened up and met Issac's gaze. "Sir, I've been working on a theory. This isn't coincidence-it's a pattern. The skull injuries are nearly identical. And every single crime scene is either abandoned or legally contested property."

Alex tapped the final image-the excavation site tied to Mr. Williams. "Even that location fits the profile. The land was under litigation for years."

"The ice factory," Issac asked, "you said it was closed-but now it's operational?"

Alex nodded. "It was a relatively minor case at the time, sir. The factory supplied ice to the local fish market. Health inspectors found they were using chemicals to make the fish appear fresher. Legal action followed, but the case didn't hold in court. The owners claimed they only produced ice-not handled the fish. During the investigation, chemicals were poured into the ground to destroy evidence, which ended up damaging the property. After the case was closed and the place was renovated, they excavated the site-and that's when the body was found."

Issac's eyes narrowed, a familiar spark igniting behind them. "Abandoned locations are only half the story, Alex. For a body to decompose, it usually takes three to four years-depending on atmospheric moisture and soil composition. But all these places you mentioned… they have water frontage, don't they?"

Alex nodded slowly.

"Moisture from nearby water would accelerate decomposition," Issac continued. "It makes identification harder. The fact that we even have identifications is surprising."

Alex looked at him, respect shining in his eyes. *This is exactly why I wanted to work with him,* he thought.

He's still sharp as hell.

Issac made his decision. "Alright, we'll start from Cochin tomorrow," he said, turning to Alex. "But tell me-what's your take on this? We can't move forward without a lead. Do you think there's any connection between the victims-something more than just the abandoned sites where they were found?"

Alex nodded thoughtfully. "I wondered the same, sir. So I dug into their backgrounds. The investigations didn't reveal any direct connections-no phone calls, no social media overlap, nothing suggesting they even knew each other. What's more, all of them had spotless reputations in their respective hometowns. Not a single hint of scandal or controversy."

"There has to be a motive behind this, Alex," Issac said. "It can't be just random killings. There's something we're missing-a thread that ties these victims together beyond just the way they died. We need to dig deeper to find it."

"Why do you think so, sir? I'm eager to hear your take," Alex asked.

Issac leaned forward. "Remember how you mentioned the skulls were viciously shattered? A random killer might strike once or twice, maybe out of panic or opportunity. But this level of damage-it suggests something else entirely. It's not just violent, it's personal."

He paused, "The fact that the forensic team couldn't recover much from the remains tells us the damage wasn't just severe-it was calculated. That's not some deranged passerby, Alex. That's someone who knew exactly what they were doing. Someone driven by deep rage-or a powerful motive."

"So, we need to identify the motive," Alex said, his voice tinged with growing excitement. "And I'm beginning to believe all these victims were connected-maybe not directly, but in some way. If we can find that link, we might uncover a common thread… something that explains why they were targeted."

"That's correct," Issac affirmed, his gaze sharpening.

"I've compiled a list of individuals we should interrogate, sir," Alex added, flipping open a notebook. "We can begin summoning them for questioning tomorrow. I've included friends, family members, and acquaintances-anyone who might've shared even a sliver of connection with the victims."

Issac nodded in agreement.

"We should make arrangements for your stay in Cochin. Do you have a place there, or will you be using the government guest house?" Issac asked.

"Actually, sir, I have a personal connection in Cochin," Alex replied with a smile. "My wife's family home is there. I'll be staying with them. Plus, she's seven months pregnant-it'll be good to spend some time with her. She'll be happy to have me around."

"Oh, nice. Congratulations to both of you," Issac said. Then, with a wry smile, he added, "Can I bum a cigarette from you?" Alex blinked, caught off guard. "Sir?"

"You said it's a stress buster," Issac said, his tone dry. "And I have a feeling we'll need plenty of them for this case."

Chapter 12
The rain begins

The deserted bus stop on the outskirts of Cochin lay shrouded in a thick, unsettling mist. The evening sky hung low with dark, brooding clouds, threatening to break at any moment. A young woman stepped off a bus and onto the wet asphalt, clutching her bag tightly. She reached for her phone and dialed.

"Mom, I just reached the stop," she said, her voice edged with exhaustion.

"Beta, do you have an umbrella? It looks like it might pour," her mother's voice came through, tight with concern.

The girl glanced up. The clouds churned overhead like a warning. "Oh no, Mamma. If it starts raining, I'll wait at George's shop. Can you send my brother with an umbrella?"

"I'll send him right away. Be careful, okay?"

"Alright. See you soon," she said, slipping the phone back into her bag.

She quickened her pace. The wind picked up, lashing her hair into a wild tangle. Lightning cracked across the sky, casting a harsh, unnatural light across the empty road. The scent of wet earth grew stronger as thunder rumbled, rolling like distant artillery fire.

Then-suddenly-a hand clamped over her mouth. She was yanked violently into the shadows.

She struggled, her screams muffled as she was dragged deeper into a vacant plot near the bus stop. The rain came down hard, drowning out every sound except the storm. Her bag hit the ground, forgotten in the mud.

By morning, news of the abduction would explode across the state, already reeling from the minister's announcement about a serial killer on the loose. For Issac and Alex, this wasn't just another case. This was a shift in the storm-one that would test their limits, unravel everything they thought they understood, and bring the killer closer to the surface than ever before.

Chapter 13
The Swamp

The next day, after Issac and Alex officially took charge of the case, grim news came in - the dead body of the abducted girl had been discovered in a swamp.

Issac immediately headed to the crime scene. On the way, he instructed the forensic team to secure the area and called Alex to check his status.

"Sir, I'm already here," Alex replied. "Questioning a few locals."

"Good work, Alex," Issac said, a flicker of approval in his voice. "I'll be there in a minute."

By the time Issac arrived, Alex had already apprehended a local farmer who'd stumbled upon the body. The man, a routine visitor to the area to collect grass for his cattle, had followed the stench of rot and found the corpse half-submerged in the muck. Seeing Issac's vehicle pull in, Alex instructed his team to take down the farmer's statement and contact details.

He walked briskly to meet Issac halfway.

"The body's in a bad state," Alex reported, "Barely recognizable. I've already secured the perimeter."

Issac gave a grim nod and stepped toward the edge of the swamp, his boots squelching in the wet ground.

Issac and Alex walked toward the body, Issac pulling on the glove Alex handed him. The stench was overwhelming, but Issac barely flinched. His eyes scanned the corpse with a seasoned gaze. The girl's clothes, torn and muddied, matched the description from the night she vanished. But it was the damage to her body that made Issac pause - chunks of flesh were missing from her thighs, the wounds ragged and raw.

Alex swallowed hard. "Stray dogs, maybe," he murmured, the words heavy with unease.

Issac rose, peeled the glove off, and the two turned away from the scene, walking in silence toward the car.

Alex broke it first. "This doesn't fit, sir. The body was left in an open swamp - not an abandoned building. This is a public spot. It contradicts the earlier pattern."

"Too early to jump the gun, Alex," Issac replied, his voice calm but sharp. "He knows we're closing in. He's changing the method to mess with us."

"Get the body sent for an emergency autopsy. I want you there personally when it's done. Also, go through all missing persons cases from this station in the last week. Cross-check dates and locations."

Alex nodded. "Understood, sir. I'm on it."

Issac gave him a final look. "I've got some homework of my own. I'll be at the office. Call me the moment they're ready with the autopsy report."

Chapter 14
The David's Star

Issac had always been drawn to the Star of David-the Magen David-though not just for its religious symbolism. To him, it was a geometric puzzle, a framework of intersecting truths. Two interlocked equilateral triangles. Sacred to some. Strategic to him.

While the world revered it as a symbol of Jewish faith and identity, Issac saw something else: tessellation-the pattern of shapes that fit together with no gaps. A concept more at home in a mathematician's thesis than a murder investigation. But in Issac's mind, the two met. In criminology, tessellation was a tool for mapping crimes, analyzing spatial data, and forecasting patterns. Issac had weaponized it.

Now, in the fading blue of early evening, he stood in his makeshift 'war' room, a dimly lit workspace carved out of what used to be his reading den. Silence hung like fog. Before him loomed a massive white Star of David etched across the wall-a canvas of calculated obsession.

He picked up the victims' photos-those Alex had laid out in clinical detail. Four murders, four crime scenes: disputed buildings, swampy ground, always close to water. Each skull had been fractured with terrifying precision. He began arranging them within the star, one at each cardinal point. Then the girl from the swamp. And now, the blank space in the center-waiting for a face that hadn't been found yet.

Issac wasn't looking for order. He was chasing something darker: the killer's rhythm. And in that rhythm, a possible next move.

His thoughts were cut short by the shrill ring of his phone.

"Tell me, Alex," he said, his voice steady but expectant.

"Sir, we've identified the body," Alex replied. "She was a staff member at a tech firm in InfoPark. The autopsy is complete, but the forensic doctor insists on meeting you in person."

Issac nodded instinctively, already reaching for his car keys. "I'll come right away. Have you informed the family?"

"Yes, sir. They're here too."

Issac hung up and stared at the star one last time. Something about the way the photos sat in those angular lines-it felt like they were waiting for him to see something.

He turned off the light, but the star glowed faintly behind him, as if still thinking.

Chapter 15
Teeth marks

As Issac arrived at the morgue, he spotted Alex gently questioning a grief-stricken couple and a young man standing beside them, hollow-eyed. Issac didn't need to ask-he already knew. Alex caught his glance and gave a discreet nod.

"Sir, that's her parents and brother," Alex whispered. "I tried, but... we're not getting much. They're too shaken for a proper statement."

Issac nodded. "Let's not drag this out. But we can't release the body until we speak to the forensic doctor. Let's meet him first."

Alex briefly stepped away and spoke to the family, requesting just a few more minutes. When he returned, his face had shifted-something else was brewing.

"Sir," he said quietly, "the girl was abducted barely five minutes from her house."

"Send her number to the cyber cell. I want the logs. And cross-reference all phones active under that cell tower when she vanished. We need traction." Issac was swift.

"On it, sir," Alex said, already committing the instructions to memory.

They entered the morgue.

The air was sharp and sterile, filled with a silence too cold for the living. Fluorescent lights buzzed faintly overhead. On the central table lay the girl's body, draped in a sheet that couldn't hide the finality beneath it. Her outline was too still, too small.

Issac greeted the forensic doctor, who looked up from a clipboard with a tired but sharp expression.

"I've heard of you, sir," the doctor said, voice low and deliberate. "And frankly, I don't think anyone else can crack this case."

Issac's eyes focused. "Tell me doc."

With a subtle gesture, the doctor invited them closer. "This is a strange one. Brutal. And deliberate." He paused, peeling back the sheet. "The skull was shattered-possibly two hours after she was already dead."

Issac felt a knot coil in his stomach as he took in the damage. The brutality was clinical, not impulsive.

"Any sign of sexual assault?" he asked, already reading the tension in the doctor's face.

The doctor shook his head slowly. "That's where it gets twisted. No sperm. No signs of penetration. But look here-" He pointed to a torn, circular wound high on the victim's thigh. "See that? Looks like an animal bite, doesn't it?"

Issac and Alex leaned in. The wound was jagged and raw.

"It's not an animal," the doctor said. "That's a human bite mark. Clean impressions. Premolars. Someone bit her... hard."

Alex recoiled, instinctively covering his mouth with a handkerchief. He turned away, eyes wide.

The doctor continued, steady as stone. "We've collected saliva from the wound. DNA results will be in by tomorrow. But I can't quite pin down the motive yet. It's... confusing. Nothing about this is typical."

Issac nodded slowly. "Doctor, I need a full report by tonight. Email it to me-include the DNA findings once they're in."

The doctor agreed with a quiet nod.

Issac and Alex walked out in silence. The cold followed them. The morgue door clicked shut behind them, but the image of the wound-and what it meant-stayed with Alex like a stain that wouldn't wash off.

Chapter 16
Teeth and Truth

Issac stood just outside the morgue, pressing his car keys to unlock the door, the air heavy with silence. His eyes locked on CI Alex, who stood a few feet away, visibly shaken.

"Convince the family that, due to the nature of the case, we can only release the body after the DNA results arrive," Issac said, voice firm but measured. "Re-question them thoroughly. And I want her call history dissected-everyone she spoke to in the days before the abduction. I want names. Context. Motive."

Alex nodded, though his face betrayed the weight he carried. The image of the bite still haunted him.

Issac's gaze narrowed. "You're not okay, are you?" he asked, tone quiet but piercing.

Alex hesitated. "Sir… this is the first time I've handled something like this. The brutality... it's hard to shake off."

Issac looked at him for a long moment, the hard edge of his experience showing. "Alex, you need to see all dead bodies as evidence. Not victims."

Alex looked up, startled by the coldness, but Issac wasn't done.

"If you let your emotions lead, you'll miss things-subtle details that hide in plain sight. That thin line between compassion and observation? You have to learn to walk it. Fast."

There was no anger in his voice, only truth.

He paused, then added, "Report to my office tomorrow with everything. I want a full breakdown. Call logs, social circle, workplace routine-every minute detail. Even the things that seem pointless. One loose thread is all we need."

Alex gave a small salute, the weight of responsibility settling deeper into his posture.

Issac held his gaze for a moment longer, then turned and walked to his car. The engine hummed to life, and the vehicle pulled away, leaving Alex behind-alone, yet already changed.

The morgue faded behind him, but the bite never did.

Chapter 17
No rape, No sperm

Issac poured himself a peg of his favorite whiskey and took a slow sip, letting the burn trace a familiar path down his throat. It was a habit he'd cultivated over the years-a ritual that marked the shift into his darker, quieter mind space. With the warmth spreading through his chest, he stepped into the shower, letting the water wash away the day's residue.

As the water coursed down his face, his mind circled back to the forensic doctor's words: "No rape. No sperm found." The phrase echoed like a refrain inside his skull. Why would someone bite into human flesh? What sort of mind did that?

The question clawed at him, until a different voice surfaced-Father Noah's, from a sermon long past: "In the last days, lawlessness will increase, and the love of many will grow cold."

The verse struck a new chord now. This case-it wasn't just savage, it felt prophetic. A darkness creeping in, not just around him, but through him. Issac stood still beneath the falling water, caught in the silence of prophecy.

Later, he poured another drink and crossed the room to his workspace. The air smelled of old paper and something faintly metallic. The 'Star of David' on the wall gleamed faintly in the low light. He stood before it, glass in hand, eyes fixed on the points. The new victim had to be placed. But where?

Just as he was about to move, his phone rang, piercing the silence. He answered.

"Sir, we've identified the skeleton found at Mr. Williams' property," came the voice on the other end.

Issac's grip tightened on the phone. "Go on."

He threw back the rest of his whiskey in a single swallow, the glass still in his hand as he listened.

"Her name was Seena. Twenty-eight. A school teacher from Kottayam-worked at a local school near her home."

"What was she doing in Trivandrum? That's over 150 kilometers away." he asked.

"We're still working on that, sir."

Issac exhaled slowly. "Find out everything. Family, friends, colleagues-dig deep. I could have sent Alex, but I need him here. Once you know more, call me."

"Understood, sir."

Issac ended the call, eyes drifting back to the star on the wall. The pattern was growing. The shadows were lengthening. And something about the shape of it all… didn't feel random anymore.

Chapter 18
A narrow escape

The evening sun cast a warm, amber glow over the isolated road as a young woman pedaled along on her bicycle. Earbuds in place, a sling bag bouncing at her side, she kept a steady pace down the deserted stretch.

Rounding a bend, she noticed a man walking straight toward her. He was tall-easily six feet-hood up, a mask covering his face. He walked down the center of the road, eyes locked on her with an unsettling stillness.

This stretch was usually empty outside peak hours. It connected the main road to Infopark, running behind a massive office complex whose tall compound walls loomed nearby like silent sentries.

Probably another health freak, she thought. *Who else would take this route on a holiday?* She stayed on her side, ignoring him-until he lunged.

In an instant, he grabbed her off the bike, lifting her like a rag doll. She kicked and thrashed, but he was too strong. Panic surged. Then instinct kicked in. Her hand dove into her sling bag, fumbling for the pepper spray.

She found it.

With a cry, she sprayed it directly into his face.

He recoiled, howling in agony as the chemical hit. She didn't wait. Grabbing her bag and the fallen bicycle, she pushed off the ground and pedaled as if her life depended on it-because it did.

When she reached the main road, heart still hammering, she spotted a highway police jeep parked near the junction. She skidded to a stop and ran toward the officers, eyes wide.

"Sir, somebody tried to mug me!" she blurted, voice shaking. "He physically attacked me!"

"What? Where did this happen?" one of the policemen asked, stepping forward.

She took a breath, steadying herself. "Behind the CSEZ building. There's a culvert-I go there often for cycling. This is the first time something like this has happened."

The officer nodded and turned to his colleague. "Inform control."

The second cop grabbed the walkie-talkie. "Control room, we have a reported mugging attempt near Infopark Police Station. Victim is female, repeat-female victim, unhurt, currently with us."

Elsewhere, Issac and Alex were traveling when their police radio crackled to life.

"The lady is unhurt and is with us now," the voice reported.

Issac snatched the radio. "This is Issac. What's your location?"

"We're at the junction near Infopark Station. Landmark is the Bharath petrol station."

"I know the spot. We're coming. Hold her if she's okay. If not, just get her details," Issac said.

He gestured to Alex, who made a sharp U-turn, flicked on the beacon lights, and accelerated.

"Copy that, sir," came the reply over the radio.

By the time Issac and Alex arrived, dusk had surrendered to a creeping darkness. Sparse streetlights threw long, uneven shadows across the road. The highway police squad waited under one such pool of light.

As Alex parked, Issac scanned the area. The roadside was wild-unmowed grass giving way to overgrown bushes, dark and tangled in the failing light. It was the kind of place that didn't just invite trouble-it stalked it.

"What made her choose this road, especially today?" he thought. "This place isn't just unsafe for a woman-it's a trap for anyone."

A highway cop approached. "Sir, she was pretty shaken. Her friends arrived, and she just wanted to leave. We let her go with them-she couldn't give a proper statement."

"But you got her contact details, right?" Alex asked, his tone sharp.

"Of course. She said she'd come to the station in the morning. Honestly, she seemed level-headed-just in shock."

"Understood," Issac nodded. "Alex, call her later. I want her in my office by 11 a.m. tomorrow."

Alex noted down the details. Issac cast one last look over the landscape. The air felt off. Something in the silence buzzed under his skin like static-unseen, but coming closer.

Chapter 19
Testosterone propionate

Issac's night was broken and restless. He tossed in bed, mind circling the attempted abduction. If confirmed, this would be the second attack since he took over the Cochin office-and far too soon. Serial offenders usually leave gaps between incidents. But this one? Two cases in a matter of days. It didn't feel random.

Unproven though it was, Issac's instincts screamed that the girl had narrowly escaped becoming the next victim. If only she could remember more-anything-that could break the silence. His reputation was already on the line, and disappointing DGP Singh wasn't an option. He had to catch the predator before another move was made.

Eventually, his thoughts blurred and faded. Sleep pulled him into a shallow, twitching REM cycle.

***

The girl arrived at Issac's office right on time. She looked tired but composed. Since Issac was out, Alex decided not to wait. She'd mentioned only having a half-day off work, so he took the lead.

He rang Issac.

"Sir, good morning. The girl's here. Only half-day leave. Want me to do a preliminary round?"

Issac's voice came through with a hint of fatigue. "Good thinking. I'm still at the location from yesterday. I'll need at least an hour to reach the office. Get what you can. I'll catch up."

Alex nodded and turned to the girl. After making sure she was settled, he began the questions.

"I take that route regularly," she began. "Past six months now-weekends and holidays only, since my schedule's packed. Usually, my friends come too, but yesterday they were out shopping for a party. I went alone for a quick ride."

She paused briefly, then continued, voice steady. "I noticed a tall guy walking toward me-hoodie, mask. Something felt off, but I stayed on my side. When I got close, he grabbed me around the waist and pulled me off the bike. We both fell. He was strong… wouldn't let go. I keep essentials in my sling bag-my friend gifted me pepper spray two days ago, for my birthday. I got it out and sprayed him straight in the face."

Alex scribbled quick notes, privately thinking: *Best birthday gift ever.*

After a few follow-up questions, he asked her to wait in the interrogation room. One of the constables brought her tea. Alex stepped out to the parking lot for a quick cigarette.

***

Meanwhile, Issac was combing through the crime scene on foot. He'd had traffic diverted early in the morning to avoid contamination. The spot behind the CSEZ building was quiet, and Issac moved methodically, trying to reconstruct the attacker's path-entry, exit, angles. His instincts-sharpened over years and Father Noah's teachings-were flaring.

Near the roadside, something caught his eye. The pepper spray. Half buried in the dirt. Just a few feet away, a small bottle glinted in the sunlight. He picked it up. A vial: Testosterone Propionate. Unopened.

Not hers, clearly. Dropped during the struggle, maybe. His brain ticked. Testosterone? Steroid? Enhancement?

Bodybuilder? Elderly man trying to boost libido? His mind made a note: ask the girl about the man's age.

At least now he had something concrete.

Then, he spotted a CCTV camera bolted to the corner of the CSEZ building. Issac cursed himself for not noticing it earlier and rushed into the CSEZ building's security office.

The footage was partial at best. The angle didn't catch the full attack. But there was a moment-just after the pepper spray-when the attacker stumbled into frame, pulling off his mask in pain. A side profile, half-shadowed. It wasn't much, but it was something.

Better than nothing, Issac thought. He left immediately.

***

Back at the office, Alex waited in the parking lot, spotting Issac's car as it arrived. Issac exited briskly, barely returning Alex's salute.

"She still here?" he asked. "Yes, sir."

"We've got something. I need to ask her a few more questions-let's go."

As they walked inside, Alex briefed him on her account. Issac listened, noting each detail with sharp, silent focus.

When they entered the waiting area, the girl was glancing nervously at her watch.

"Sir, I'm getting late for work," she said, standing.

"Don't worry," Issac replied calmly. "I'll speak to your HR if needed. Right now, we need your help."

She hesitated, then nodded.

In the briefing room, Issac played the CCTV clip. The girl on screen, cycling with calm purpose. Then a cut, a blank, and suddenly-the attacker. Recoiling, clawing at his face, tearing off his mask. His expression contorted in pain, then gone. A few seconds later, she appeared again, speeding out of frame, face wild with panic.

She froze watching it.

"Do you remember anything else?" Issac asked. "His face?"

She didn't move at first. Then: "He had a mask when he grabbed me. But his eyes... I remember his eyes."

Issac turned to Alex, energized. "We have a side profile. Think our sketch artist can build from it?"

Alex nodded. "Absolutely."

"Take her to the artist. Once done, have the sketch mailed to me. Then drop her at her office-get her leave sorted if needed."

"Yes, sir," Alex said.

The girl stood slowly, trauma still ghosting behind her eyes. She followed Alex out, one step at a time, as Issac remained behind-staring at the freeze-frame of the attacker's partial face, burned into shadow.

But now, at last, the shadows had a shape.

Chapter 20
But he is dead

The sketch artist had done a commendable job bringing the attacker's features to life with the limited information available. As instructed, Alex sent the completed sketch to Issac, who took a printout along with several copies.

Issac's experience with the State Crime Records Bureau (SCRB) now proved invaluable. He tapped into his old network, sharing the sketch across departments and seeking help in identifying the man behind the image. His calls were swift, targeted, and purposeful-each copy of the sketch moving like bait into the hands of trusted officers.

While buried in cross-referencing databases, Issac's focus was broken by a call from reception.

"Sir, a Circle Inspector wants to meet you. Says it's urgent."

He hesitated, slightly annoyed at the interruption-but gave the nod. "Send him in."

A tall, dark-uniformed officer stepped inside with a measured presence.

"Sir, I'm Circle Inspector Omar. I served as jailor at the Central Jail in Viyoor."

Issac's interest was piqued. He gestured for him to sit.

"I heard you're back in the crime division," Omar continued, "and that you're heading the serial killer case. I have some information... might not seem explosive, but I believe it's relevant."

Issac leaned back, his eyes narrowing slightly as he studied the man. "Go on."

"Ten years ago, we had an inmate," Omar said carefully. "He used a pattern almost identical to this. He was known inside as 'The Ripper.'"

Issac sat up. His voice was sharper now. "You're serious?"

Omar nodded. "He was like a wild animal. Unpredictable. Violent. Kept in chains. Solitary confinement only. No staff wanted to deal with him. I'll be honest-I was scared of him. And that wasn't normal for me."

Issac leaned forward, something electric behind his stillness.

"He would rape the victims even after death," Omar continued. "He crushed their skulls. Brutal. And methodical."

Without a word, Issac reached into his file and pulled out the sketch. He slid it across the table to Omar.

"Is this him?"

Omar looked down-and froze. His face drained. He stared at the sketch, eyes scanning every curve of the jawline, the mouth, and the unmistakable eyes.

"It looks like him… The lips, the stare. But the hair was longer back then. We couldn't get him to trim it. Always had chains on. This one's got short hair, a thin mustache, stubble…"

Issac didn't hesitate. "It's him. I'm sure of it."

But Omar leaned back, suddenly distant. "No, sir. It can't be."

Issac's eyes narrowed. "Why not?"

Omar exhaled slowly. "Because he was hanged five years ago. Capital punishment. No family came for the body-it was donated to the medical college for dissection. I personally signed the transfer papers."

Issac stared at him. The air turned still. "…What?" he asked.

A single word, stretched tight across the silence.

Chapter 21
Dead Men Don't Run

"What?" DGP Singh said, his voice sharp with disbelief, mirroring Issac's own reaction just hours ago. "You're saying the man we're after was hanged five years ago?"

"I know how it sounds, sir," Issac replied, steady. "But the sketch is real. Based on CCTV footage. Eyewitness confirmed it. There's no mistake-someone out there looks exactly like the Ripper."

Singh sighed heavily. "I can't wrap my head around this, Issac. It's too much."

"There's a mystery here," Issac said. "And we're going to crack it."

"But how, Issac?" Singh snapped. "How the hell do we chase a man who's supposed to be dead?"

Issac didn't blink. "This sketch came from evidence. Concrete sources. Either it's a lookalike, or someone deliberately wants us to think the Ripper never died. Either way, it's our best lead."

Singh paused. Then, calmer: "Could it be coincidence? Some genetic match? A twin? A doppelgänger? Whatever it is, we should issue a lookout notice immediately."

"Not yet, sir," Issac said firmly. "If we go public and the media spots the resemblance, the Chief Minister will panic. The moment this hits the news, we lose control of the narrative."

Singh nodded, weighing the implications. "Then what's your plan?"

Issac leaned forward, lowering his voice. "There's a discrepancy in the crimes. The Ripper-he was all about control and sexual violence. He raped his victims, even after death. But the last girl? No signs of rape. Only brutality. That tells me this isn't the same person... at least not completely."

Singh was quiet, processing.

"I want to investigate the Ripper's past," Issac continued. "We know too little about him. He came from a village called Kuldhara in Rajasthan. I'm flying to Jodhpur tomorrow. I've already connected with their crime division-they'll assist me on the ground."

Singh's tone shifted-confidence replacing concern. "Very good, Issac. I trust you'll find something. Are you taking Alex with you?"

Issac shook his head. "No, sir. I've assigned him something specific. He'll stay back and handle it."

With that, Issac took his leave.

He had a name. A village. A dead man whose shadow had started walking again.

Chapter 22
Twins in the frame

At the Jodhpur Crime Department, Issac was greeted warmly by Mr. Sharma. After the initial formalities, they got straight to the point.

"Sir, I've reviewed the data you sent," Sharma began. "It seems the individual in question can't be from Kuldhara directly. Most likely, he's from a nearby village. Kuldhara itself has been abandoned for years."

"Why?" Issac asked. "Famine?"

"No, sir," Sharma replied. "Kuldhara's got a strange history. It's considered a ghost village. According to local legends, the Paliwal Brahmins cursed it in the early 1800s after a dispute with a minister. They left overnight, and the rest of the residents followed soon after."

Issac leaned in slightly. "And now?"

"It's completely uninhabited," Sharma said. "Mostly used by filmmakers and photographers these days. Our databases don't have any usable records on it."

"Can't we go there and make some inquiries?" Issac asked.

Sharma shook his head. "There's no one left to ask. The surrounding villages have dwindled too. In the '80s and '90s, missionaries came in-offered education. Most people moved out after, scattered across Rajasthan."

Issac's voice was laced with hope. "There must be something. Records, documents… anything?"

"We sent a team to Jaisalmer-nearest town, around 17 kilometers from Kuldhara. They canvassed the panchayats and government offices. Came back

Empty-handed."

Disappointment flickered across Issac's face. He'd traveled a long way for a dead end. But a part of him still wanted to see it for himself. Even an abandoned place held echoes.

Just then, Sharma spoke again. "We did find one thing. An old photograph taken by the missionaries."

He handed Issac a faded picture. A local family stood with a few missionaries. At the edge were two children-a boy and a girl, around ten years old. Twins.

"This was taken just before the missionaries left," Sharma said. "The man and woman in the photo? They were later found dead. In Kuldhara. Under mysterious circumstances."

Issac's eyes narrowed, focused on the children.

"Let me guess," he said softly. "Their skulls were shattered."

Sharma looked stunned. "Yes. But… how did you know?"

Issac didn't answer directly. "Because crime often follows a familiar script. Can I take this photo with me? Or can you send me a digital copy?"

"We need it for our records," Sharma replied. "But I'll email you a high-res scan."

Issac nodded, still staring at the twins. "I'm taking the next flight out. Thank you, Mr. Sharma. This was helpful."

***

On the way to the airport, Issac called Alex.

"Alex, I'm sending you a photo. Two children in it-twins. Give it to our cyber team. Ask them to

Enhance it using AI. I want to see how they'd look today."

"You sound like you've got something, sir," Alex replied, alert.

"I do. I'll explain everything once I land. Also, we're meeting the girl again tomorrow. At her office. I want her to see the enhanced photo. Maybe something will click."

"Understood, sir. Have a safe flight."

As the call ended, Alex leaned back, piecing it together. Issac had mentioned twins.

Chapter 23
Flat chest, Sharp nails

Issac and Alex met Nayana at her office cafeteria. She was on probation and couldn't take leave, but Issac had personally intervened with HR to get her a few hours off. The gesture wasn't just kindness-it was calculated. If she felt at ease, she might remember more.

"Thank you both," Nayana said, settling into the chair opposite them. "I really appreciate what you did."

Issac gave a small nod. "We're just trying to help."

He leaned in slightly, keeping his tone casual. "Nayana, did you notice anything unusual about the person who attacked you? Anything that didn't quite add up?"

She looked hesitant. "Sir, I don't know what you mean exactly. Are you looking for something specific?"

Issac smiled faintly. "Just reconfirming something basic. You're sure it was a man who attacked you?"

She hesitated again. "He was very strong," she said, then added quietly, "And flat-chested... I don't think a girl could've picked me up like that."

"Good enough," Issac said, eyes locked on hers.

"You must've seen something when you pepper-sprayed him. A glimpse of his face, maybe?"

Nayana nodded.

Issac glanced at Alex, who took out the tablet and brought up the AI-enhanced image-an adult male and female, digitally aged from an old photo. He handed it to Nayana. Both men watched her reaction closely.

"Do either of these people look familiar?" Issac asked, voice low.

Nayana stared at the screen. After a moment, she pointed to the male.

"Yes," she said. "But… he didn't have this thick a moustache. It was more like baby hair. Not even stubble."

She leaned closer. "And I think he was bald-or had a shaved head. I'm not entirely sure."

Her brow furrowed in concentration, fingers tightening around the tablet. Then, almost to herself, she added, "And sharp nails."

Issac leaned forward. "Nails?"

"When I showered that evening, my skin burned. That's when I noticed… scratch marks. Long ones. His nails were sharp. They cut me."

Her voice cracked slightly as she added, "They were deep."

Issac didn't speak right away. He just nodded.

"Thank you, Nayana. This was helpful," he said finally, rising to his feet. Alex followed.

Nayana looked up at them, her voice trembling slightly. "Please catch him, sir. Before someone else goes through what I did."

Issac met her gaze and shook her hand. "We will," he said. "I promise."

Chapter 24
The Other Twin

"Sir, I'm totally confused," Alex said, frustration spilling into his voice as they walked toward the car. "The guy was hanged. Dead. But Nayana says it's him who attacked her. How do we go after someone who's already gone?"

Issac didn't even glance at him. "Who said we're pursuing him, Alex?"

Alex blinked. "Sir?"

Issac stopped, turning to face him. "I thought you'd have figured it out by now. We're not after the male in the photo."

Alex stared. "Then who-?" "The female."

Alex's mouth went dry. "What?"

Issac stepped closer, voice low but deliberate. "Think, Alex. The strength to lift Nayana. The baby moustache. The stubble. The vial of testosterone we found at the crime scene. That bottle didn't belong to a man. It belonged to her."

Alex's breath caught. "But... testosterone's a male hormone, right?"

"Yes," Issac replied. "But it's used for many things. Older men take it for libido or therapy. TRT, they call it. But in females? It's naturally produced, but only a fraction compared to men. When a woman supplements it, her body changes-facial hair, increased strength, muscle definition."

Alex was quiet, the puzzle pieces clattering into place.

"You've seen female bodybuilders?" Issac added. "Some with extremely masculine builds. That's often testosterone. Steroids. Most won't admit it, but it's there."

Alex finally exhaled. "So that explains the hair… and the strength."

"And the scratches," Issac said, flatly. "We're not just dealing with a woman on hormones. We're dealing with someone possibly delusional-someone who might not accept their own identity."

Alex nodded slowly, the realization sinking in.

"We're not chasing the Ripper," Issac said. "We're chasing the other twin."

They reached the office. Issac's face hardened, his voice suddenly brisk.

"Get a team ready. Meet me in my cabin. We're in for some sleepless nights."

Chapter 25
She?

Issac held up the unused bottle of testosterone before his team. "This is no ordinary clue," he began. "Testosterone Propionate. Typically used by men undergoing TRT or by female bodybuilders. But in our case, it narrows the field-significantly."

He walked slowly in front of them, eyes sharp. "A woman using this medication will eventually need to replenish her supply. That's our window. Most small pharmacies don't stock it regularly-so focus on the bigger players in the city. Quietly get customer logs. Recent buyers. Prescriptions. Card payments. Anything."

He paused, letting it sink in.

"She may look traditionally feminine, or appear masculine like during the Nayana attack. We don't know how she presents day to day, so don't rely on appearances. What we do know is-this is her trail. We follow it."

One of the officers raised a hand. "Sir… if she's presenting male and buying a hormone usually associated with men, will that raise any flags?"

Issac nodded. "Exactly. Which is why we'll notify pharmacies discreetly. No media. No chatter."

He turned serious. "Also, do not-under any circumstances-mention to anyone that we're tracking a female suspect. Not even internally. The legal terrain is complicated, and this case is already on thin ice. Keep it tight. Keep it quiet."

His voice lowered.

"This one's smart. And fast. But we've got the edge now."

Issac's instincts were right. The person they were pursuing was indeed the Ripper's sister.

Whatever had happened in the ghost villages of Kuldhara and beyond-the trauma, the abandonment, the superstition-had carved deep into both siblings. One was executed. The other had learned how to disappear in plain sight.

Now, she was moving again.

And Issac had no intention of letting her vanish twice.

Chapter 26
She was here!!

Alex and his team began their search, focusing on major pharmacies as per Issac's instructions. Alex took charge of the InfoPark sector, scouring the chain outlets around the tech hub. As they moved deeper, past the towering glass buildings, the landscape shifted-rubber estates flanked underdeveloped roads, and the concrete pulse of the city gave way to rural quiet.

One pharmacy stood out. It straddled the last two phases of InfoPark and sat alone in the middle of Phase Three and four-always busy, always watching.

Inside, Alex approached the cashier and showed him two photos: one of a woman in traditional attire, the other a figure in a hoodie and mask. The cashier barely glanced at the first, but his eyes lingered on the second. A flicker of recognition.

"He was here ten minutes ago," the cashier said. "Left in a hurry."

Alex's eyes shot up to the ceiling camera. "Is the CCTV working?"

The cashier nodded.

"Secure the footage," Alex barked at his colleague.

"He looked...off," the cashier added. "Red eyes. Kept fidgeting. Paid with tens and twenties. Loose change."

Alex rushed outside. Two roads split ahead-one leading back to the city, the other towards the outskirts. His instinct said left, but a cluster of auto-rickshaws caught his eye near the corner.

He approached fast, flashing his ID. "Circle Inspector Alex. Anyone seen this person?" he asked, showing the masked photo.

The drivers straightened. One spoke up quickly. "Yes, sir! He got into Ben's auto."

Alex leaned in. "You're sure?"

"Positive. I was next after Ben in the line." "Anyone have Ben's number?"

"We all do, sir."

Alex snapped, "Call him. Now."

The driver fumbled with his phone and dialed. "Ben, where are you?"

"I'm on my way back to the stand, why?" came the answer.

Alex grabbed the phone. "This is Circle Inspector Alex. Don't panic."

"I swear, sir-I didn't do anything!" Ben stammered. "We know. Just tell me-where did you drop him?" "At the market, sir."

"Listen carefully. Come back here. Don't talk to anyone, don't answer any other calls."

Just then, Alex's colleague returned, breathless. "Got the footage. It's him. Positive match."

Alex didn't waste time. He dialed Issac.

"Sir, we've got a hit. She's at the InfoPark market. Sending location now."

"Good work, Alex," Issac said, excitement in his voice. "Get there. Don't use the police jeep."

"I can take an auto. I'm already at the stand." "Perfect. You in uniform?"

"Just trousers and shoes."

"Change the shoes. Borrow a uniform if needed. Go as a driver. Send me your live location. Wait for me before you move in."

Alex nodded, already moving. He borrowed a shirt from one of the drivers and switched into sandals. In moments, he was behind the wheel of an auto-rickshaw, blending in. His colleague climbed into another auto behind him.

Engines roared. The hunt was on.

Chapter 27
Seal the Leaks

Before heading out to join Alex, Issac briefed DGP Singh over the phone, his tone clipped and controlled. He requested absolute discretion until further notice, aware of the legal landmines they were stepping over.

Singh raised the obvious point. "If this goes public, we'll need female officers on the ground. You know the rules."

Issac had already considered it. "Not a problem-as long as we don't reveal her identity until she's in custody. Nayana's testimony can confirm it. You've always said the end justifies the means, sir."

It was a gamble, but one Issac was willing to take.

What bothered him more was Singh's proximity to the Chief Minister. That man had a chronic habit of leaking sensitive information-sometimes out of carelessness, sometimes for leverage. Neither option helped.

Everything collapses if the media even smells this operation, Issac thought, ending the call without further debate.

He threw the phone onto the passenger seat and started the engine. The road ahead was clear, but the stakes had never felt heavier.

Alex and his team had done the unthinkable-found the woman faster than expected. Now it was up to Issac to make sure she didn't vanish again.

Chapter 28
The Passenger

Alex quickly slipped into the borrowed uniform shirt, blending in like any other driver. He motioned to the auto owner to follow with his colleague in another vehicle. As they approached the market, luck tipped in their favor-the woman was exiting, scanning the road for a ride.

She raised her hand and flagged Alex down, unaware of who he really was. "Can you take me to Kottachira, outskirts side?" she asked, her voice low and husky-feminine, but unusually deep.

Alex nodded casually. "Where's that? I don't go that way much."

"I'll give you the directions," she muttered.

Alex played the part to perfection, haggling over the return fare like any street-savvy auto driver. "That's far. Got to come back empty. Four hundred minimum."

"Three-fifty," she countered.

"Three hundred and seventy not a rupee less," he shot back, final.

She climbed in.

Alex glanced at the rearview mirror once before pulling off. He prayed Issac would reach in time, but the road was narrowing, both literally and tactically. If Issac's police vehicle showed up too soon, she might bolt. Taking her in the crowded market would've been chaos. Better to find where she stayed. Better to wait for the right moment.

From a few vehicles behind, Alex's colleague followed discreetly in the second auto. He kept Issac updated in real-time, advising silence-no calls to Alex, nothing that could tip her off.

They left the city behind, turning down a road that cut through the belly of the rubber belt. Lush groves flanked both sides. The asphalt cracked and vanished in parts.

Alex tried small talk, griping about the roads. "They fix only main roads and forget the rest... Typical."

She grunted. "Hmm."

No warmth. No trust. Her replies were tight-lipped. Her smell filled the auto-raw meat from her shopping bag, stale sweat, unwashed fabric. The air turned heavy.

Alex noted it all. The way her hoodie barely hid her tension. The way she kept looking over her shoulder.

Soon, she directed him off the main road. "Turn there." He obeyed.

The auto rolled up to the edge of a vast rubber estate. Half-wild, half-farmed. She pointed to a path. At the end, a broken-down structure stood crooked-an old tapping quarters, maybe. Forgotten. Half-swallowed by weeds and rust.

Alex pulled the brake and tapped the meter. "Three hundred and seventy"

She pulled out a wad of crumpled notes, dirt-stained and damp. Her nails were chipped and packed with grime. Alex took the money with a calm hand, but his eyes flicked across the plantation. No movement. No sound. It wasn't tapping season. The place was perfect-isolated, abandoned, easy to disappear into.

He turned the auto back toward the road, slow and steady.

Issac would be here soon.

Chapter 29
The Quiet Storm

Issac tracked Alex's GPS and met him near the rubber plantation. He parked his vehicle well out of sight, killing the engine early to avoid alerting the target. The path ahead was silent, thick with trees and the faint rustle of dry leaves.

Alex crouched near the roadside and drew a crude map in the dirt with a twig, sketching the layout of the hideout-a single-room structure, one front door, one exit in the back, flanked by dense growth.

Issac studied it and nodded. "I'll take the front. You circle around. Have the others cover both flanks. If she runs, aim below the knees."

Alex added, "Move quiet. No dry leaves."

With roles set, they crept toward the hideout-silent, surgical.

Once the perimeter was covered, they waited. Issac knelt near the front door, eye to the keyhole. Inside, the woman had removed her hoodie. Her upper body was bare except for a sports bra, and a prominent surgical scar ran diagonally across her chest-a clean incision from a breast removal procedure. She moved methodically, stoking a small fire under a metal plate and cooking meat over a makeshift burner.

Issac exhaled once. This was the moment.

He rose and kicked the door with force-not just to gain entry, but to signal the team.

The sound exploded through the silence.

She flinched, startled, but recovered instantly and darted for the rear exit. But Alex was already there-his boot had smashed through the weakened door just seconds earlier. A loose wooden plank, jagged and swinging, struck her in the side, sending her sprawling.

She landed hard but rolled fast, hand snatching a nearby knife. She lunged at Issac with a wild swing.

He dodged easily, her form reckless and unbalanced. That gave him the opening.

One swift slap across both ears-hard, precise. The blow disoriented her instantly, a wave of pain and pressure knocking her back into the dirt.

She collapsed.

Alex and the others rushed in, efficient and silent. They bound her wrists, pulled the hoodie over her again, and covered her face. No screams. No drama.

Just business. Within minutes, she was secured in the back seat of the car. The team pulled out, heading straight for the interrogation quarters-no sirens, no radio chatter.

Chapter 30
The Big mouth

Issac called DGP Singh the moment the suspect was secured. "She's in custody. We're taking her to the interrogation center now."

There was a pause-then a breath of relief.

"Well done, Issac," Singh said, his voice full of unfiltered pride. "You've done it again. Knew I could count on my best man."

For a moment, Issac let the words hang. The chase was over, but something in his gut refused to rest.

Back at headquarters, Singh couldn't contain his excitement. He dialed the Chief Minister almost immediately, eager to share the victory. But in his enthusiasm, he fumbled the details.

"We've apprehended the suspect," he said. "Turns out... it's a transgender woman."

The Chief Minister latched onto the word like a shark catching scent. The opportunity was too ripe. Within the hour, he was in front of cameras, capitalizing on the moment.

"Our police department has successfully apprehended the transgender individual who had been terrorizing Cochin," he declared, face stoic, voice full of fire.

Reporters pounced.

"Is this another feather in your cap, sir?"

The Chief Minister snapped. "To hell with the feather-and the crown."

He leaned forward into the mic, his tone turning acidic. "You people teamed up with the opposition to tear me down, demanding resignations when you should've been supporting the department. This is the result of leadership. This is how we keep people safe."

He paused, letting the tension crackle across airwaves.

"The police force under me is at its best. We've built trust. We've delivered results. And we'll continue to do so."

He ended the interview with a smug smile and a final nod to the cameras.

Issac caught a criminal, the minister caught a head line.

Chapter 31
The press 'MEAT'!

Outside the interrogation center, a crowd had already formed-reporters, photographers, and curious onlookers hungry for answers. News of the arrest had gone viral within the hour.

DGP Singh and ADGP Khanna pushed through the sea of cameras, flashing lights slicing through the dusk. The headlines all screamed the same phrase: *"Transgender Serial Killer Caught"*. But the cracks were already showing.

Nayana, the survivor, had referred to her attacker as "he" in her social media posts. The AI sketch that led to the arrest matched the person in custody, but questions were multiplying by the minute.

The media pounced.

"Sir, have you confirmed that this person is the serial killer?"

"Is it true the individual is transgender? And if so, how was the arrest made without a female officer present?"

"When will he be taken to the magistrate?"

"The victim identified a male. So why are you spinning this as a transgender arrest? Are you trying to divert public attention?"

That last question carried weight. It had a tone-one that hinted at politics, maybe even planted by the opposition.

DGP Singh raised a hand. "Please, hold your peace and give us time. The individual was apprehended just an hour ago and will be presented before a magistrate soon."

He paused, deliberately avoiding the word

transgender, aware of the minefield it represented-both legally under the Transgender Persons (Protection of Rights) Act, 2019, and socially in a state already on edge.

"We'll provide a formal briefing by morning. Until then, I urge the media not to spread unverified information. We need to handle this responsibly."

Without waiting for follow-ups, Singh and Khanna stepped through the compound gates and shut the noise behind them.

Inside, Issac was waiting.

Chapter 32
Oops!!

Inside the interrogation room, Issac and Alex did everything by the book-and a few things outside it-to get her to talk. A few female officers stood by, ensuring protocol was followed. But she remained silent. Even when physical discomfort was applied, she didn't flinch. Just stared.

Eventually, they stopped. She lay on the floor, exhausted, eyes dull but burning underneath.

"Sir, she hasn't said a word," Alex muttered. "I'm worried we might be crossing a line."

"If the DNA doesn't match, we'll have no legal ground left," Issac replied. "But don't worry-it will match. Did you inform Nayana for the identification?"

"She's on her way, sir."

They stepped out and poured themselves black coffee, steam rising in the flickering tube light.

ADGP Khanna and DGP Singh entered the hallway. Both wore the same question on their faces.

"Issac, what do we have so far?" Khanna asked.

"Nothing conclusive," Issac admitted. "We've sent saliva and dental samples for DNA matching. Nayana's arriving soon to confirm identity. But we need time-buy us some from the magistrate. The link to the five previous murders isn't airtight yet."

Khanna frowned. "Random victims, you think?"

"Most likely," Issac replied. "But that doesn't clear her yet."

Just then, a junior officer stepped in. "Sir, a doctor's here to see you. Says it's urgent." Issac nodded. "Send him in."

A tall, well-kept man walked in, flashing an ID. "Dr. Mathew Zachariah. I'm head of psychiatry at Trivandrum Mental Health Centre."

"You wanted to meet me?" Issac asked.

"Yes. The woman you've arrested is one of my patients. She was locked in an isolation cell for over four years due to violent behavior. Two months ago, she showed signs of improvement, so we moved her to the general ward. She escaped. We've had an FIR filed since the day she disappeared."

Everyone in the room froze.

"Locked up for four years?" Singh repeated, stunned.

"Four and a half," Dr. Zachariah corrected. "We have complete records. I'm not here to defend her, but if she was locked up that long, she couldn't have committed the five murders."

"How did she even end up there?" Khanna asked.

"She got into a bar fight. The police couldn't control her-had to sedate her. The court sent her to us for psychiatric treatment. Her behavior was unpredictable. She had to be isolated."

Alex stepped forward. "What if Nayana identifies her as the same person who tried to abduct her?"

"Then she goes back to the hospital. Legally, she's a patient. But you have a bigger problem now."

Issac narrowed his eyes. "What problem?"

The doctor exhaled. "The media's running with the 'transgender' label, thanks to the Minister's statement.

But she's not transgender. She exhibits lesbian traits. She had her breasts removed via surgery, probably with a forged prescription for testosterone. That explains her deep voice and facial hair. When the hormone levels crash, it causes severe chemical imbalance-mood swings, aggression, even psychotic breaks."

Alex's eyes widened. "That explains the last murder."

Dr. Zachariah nodded. "Yes. But with this media frenzy, the Human Rights Commission will intervene. They always do when identity is misrepresented. And they're relentless."

Singh groaned. "Oh, tell me about it."

He turned to Issac, who hadn't said a word in a while. "Issac... looks like we're in deep trouble."

Issac sipped his coffee, eyes locked on the interrogation room door.

"I don't think so," he said quietly. "Not yet."

Chapter 33
Hand it Over!

The Minister's loose lips had set off a firestorm. His careless use of the word *"transgender"* had sparked outrage from the LGBTQ+ community and handed the opposition exactly what they needed-a controversy wrapped in identity politics.

Headlines exploded.

"Minister Weaponizes Gender for Political Cover-Up"

"Transgender Outrage: Demand for Apology and Resignation"

"Scapegoat or Serial Killer?"

Facing mounting pressure, the Minister paced behind his desk, seething.

"This is all your fault!" he roared at DGP Singh and Issac. "If you had controlled the narrative, none of this would've happened. Now I have no choice but to hand it over to the CBI. I'll move it to cabinet tomorrow."

Issac didn't flinch. "Sir, we stopped a serial killing spree. If we hadn't caught her, more women would be dead. Can't you lead with that?"

The Minister slammed his palm on the table. "Don't you know how the media works here? They've already joined hands with the opposition. They're not looking for facts-they want blood. I need to save face. My decision is final. You're dismissed."

That was it. No debate. No nuance. Just a political equation to solve.

By the next morning, the cabinet approval was in motion. The order was signed. Issac received the directive in his inbox-formally requesting full handover of all investigation files, evidence logs, and forensic reports to the Central Bureau of Investigation.

The city braced itself for more chaos. Between the police pulling back and the CBI's eventual arrival, the cracks in law and order widened. Rumors spread. Social media spun theories. Trust wavered.

And while the media hunted headlines, demolition crews were setting charges at an old colonial ruin on the city's edge-just another quiet item on the government's list.

The case was no longer just a murder investigation. It was political currency.

And something buried was about to rise.

Chapter 34
The sixth!!

The Viceroy House stood on the city's forgotten edge, cloaked in history and moss. Once a grand estate reserved for British viceroys, it had long since slipped into decay. The artificial lake out front now shimmered with algae. The manicured grounds had surrendered to weeds and silence.

After passing through various private hands, the property was finally claimed by the government. The plan: turn the place into a public park, complete with a boathouse, restaurants, and walking paths. A contractor with ties to Mr. Williams-the senior political figure mired in previous controversy-had secured one of the main tenders.

Some conservationists pushed to preserve the site as a heritage landmark, but the structure's state was too far gone. Climate, rot, and years of neglect had left the walls brittle and unsafe. The compromise: retain what little could be salvaged, demolish the rest with minimal dynamite.

The demolition was scheduled for the day after Issac's removal from the serial killer case. The timing wasn't lost on anyone. The Chief Minister was under fire, the opposition relentless in their calls for his resignation. In response, he'd played his trump card-demanding a CBI probe and promising full transparency. Anything to survive another scandal.

At the site, demolition workers and news crews milled about under a hazy sky. Police secured the perimeter. Reporters leaned into cameras, narrating the moment.

"This colonial relic," one anchor said, "will soon be reborn into something the people can actually

Use-thanks to this administration's vision."

Another, less aligned, muttered, "Curious amount of security for an empty building... unless there's something they're not telling us."

Then it happened.

A policeman burst from the building, eyes wide, muttering something into his superior's ear. The officer nodded sharply and rushed inside. The media smelled blood. Cameras followed.

Inside, demolition workers were marking blast points when one of them struck something-hard.

It wasn't rock. As the dirt was cleared, the shape became horrifyingly clear: a human leg, curled beneath layers of packed earth and concrete dust. Flesh. Bone. Decomposition.

The officer stared in disbelief. Outside, the feed was already live. Within minutes, it was everywhere:

"HUMAN REMAINS FOUND AT VICEROY DEMOLITION SITE"

"PARK PROJECT HALTED AS GRISLY DISCOVERY SHOCKS STATE"

Just as the headlines about Issac's removal were fading…

The dead had started talking again.

Chapter 35
I'm not done!!

The discovery of the sixth body-same signature brutality, same waterfront burial-added fuel to the Chief Minister's push for a full CBI probe. Cameras rolled, hashtags trended, and just like that, the spotlight shifted.

Though officially removed from the case, Alex made his way to the site. The moment he saw the corpse, his heart sank. The skull was split clean from forehead to nape-just like the others. Flesh pale. Bones exposed. Water lapping in the distance.

But this victim was different.

He was male. Half-naked. Found only in his underwear. No ID. No clothes.

Alex called Issac immediately. "Same skull fracture," he said. "But the body's male… and stripped."

There was silence on the other end. No questions. No theories.

Just silence.

Alex could feel it-Issac's disappointment, heavier than any verdict. He tried to fill the void with optimism, but Issac only muttered something unintelligible before ending the call.

Later that evening, the headlines erupted again. Political vultures circled.

Some called it a disgrace. Others blamed Kerala Police, asking if Issac was ever the right man for the job. A few loyal voices argued he'd been robbed of time-his 100% success rate should've bought him more.

At the police club, over untouched food and bitter coffee, DGP Singh sat across from a restless Issac.

"What can we do, Issac?" Singh asked gently. "Be glad it's not our headache anymore. Don't take it personally."

Issac finally spoke. "Sir, I'm not personalizing it. I'm defending my record. You know what that means to me. Isn't that why you called me in the first place?"

Singh nodded slowly. "Yes… but there's nothing we can do."

Issac stared at him-sharp, unwavering. The DGP knew that look.

"What?" Singh asked.

"Give me permission to investigate-unofficially," Issac said, his voice low, calm, and immovable.

"No way," Singh replied, almost instinctively. "That's a protocol breach."

Issac leaned back, his tone edged with a smirk. "Since when do you care about protocols? I'm not asking for orders. Just a little blindness."

Singh sighed. "Worst case? You get suspended for two months. No official paper trail, I'm in the clear. But you'll have to be invisible. No noise. No heat."

Issac simply nodded. "Thank you." He got up to leave.

"Wait," Singh said, resigned. "One more thing. A lead, maybe. Remember Seena-the teacher from Kottayam? When she went missing, a café owner claimed she regularly met someone at his place. Café shut down, guy moved to Dubai. But he's in town right now. "I'll WhatsApp you the details. Quietly follow it up."

Issac gave him a crisp nod. "Understood, sir."

Chapter 36
So is mine

Sarah didn't walk into rooms-she cut through them.

Forty, with the posture of a soldier and the eyes of someone who'd seen what others flinched to imagine. Athletic, sharp-jawed, unflinching. Every move calculated. Every word, deliberate.

She stepped off the flight and went straight to the CBI's Cochin office. No check-in. No coffee. No downtime.

Joint Director Mehra met her at the door. "Welcome to Cochin, Sarah. How was the flight?

Sarah didn't blink. "Late. Foggy. Packed with frustrated fliers and crew trying to hold it together. Not my idea of a soft landing."

Mehra chuckled lightly. "Sounds like a typical day at Delhi airport. You should get some rest at the guest house."

"I didn't come to rest," she replied. "Is my team ready?"

"Yes, of course. Conference hall's prepped. They've been waiting for you."

She nodded once and started walking.

Sarah had reviewed the case files on the flight. Her team was handpicked:

VK, an ethical hacker who ignored red tape like it didn't exist.

Shanu, PhD in Criminology-quick, clinical, and sharp-eyed.

JD, a local CBI officer. Young, objective, no baggage.

As Sarah entered the conference hall, conversation died. They weren't expecting her to look like that-and certainly not to carry that kind of presence.

"Team," Mehra began, "this is Sarah, from the Delhi office. She'll be leading the investigation."

He pointed. "VK… your hacker. Best we've got when it comes to systems and surveillance."

VK stood. "Ma'am." "Sarah," she corrected.

"Yes, Sarah," he said quickly.

"This is Shanu," Mehra continued. "Criminologist. Worked on multiple joint ops with Kerala Cyber Cell. Sharpest eyes in the room."

"Pleasure," Shanu said, offering a polite nod. "We, uh, tried Googling you. Found a lot about your cases. No photos, though."

Sarah's tone was flat. "I was with RAW. Hence im low key."

That answered everything.

"This is JD," Mehra added. "One of ours. Fresh, smart, clean instincts."

"Looking forward to working with you, ma'am," JD said. Sarah glanced at him. "Let's see how long that lasts."

Mehra cleared his throat and shifted tone. "Look, I'll be honest with you, Sarah, Officer Issac-he was on the right track. The man's brilliant. His track record's spotless. Every case he's handled, he's cracked. Hundred percent success.

Sarah cut in, calm and firm. "So is mine."

Mehra raised his brows, then nodded with a tight smile. He glanced at his watch. "The guest house is ready. Official vehicle's parked downstairs. Driver included."

"No driver." "You sure?"

"Yes, we will drive."

He didn't press it. "Alright. And in case you need local support, police assistance is available."

"That, won't be necessary."

Mehra gave her a longer look this time, then turned to the team. "Well, you're in good hands now. Best of luck."

As he left, Shanu leaned toward VK and muttered, "This woman's got attitude."

Sarah heard it. She didn't turn-just smiled faintly.

Once they were alone, Sarah faced her team. "I'm up to speed till yesterday. What's new?"

Shanu replied first. "Still waiting on the DNA results from the body found at Viceroy House. I've been following up with the lab."

"There's one angle the local police didn't follow through on," JD added. "A café owner. He gave a statement when that teacher, Seena, went missing. Said she used to meet someone at his place pretty regularly."

"Issac missed that?" Sarah asked, eyebrow raised.

"Not really," JD said. "When they recorded the statement she was just a missing person. Her body turned up later-at Mr. Williams' property." Sarah processed that with a single nod. "We meet him tomorrow."

She didn't need to say anything else. The Bureau had officially entered the game.

Chapter 37
They're all dead!!

When Sarah and her team arrived at the café owner's house, he welcomed them with mild unease. His café, he explained, used to sit near a school and college-mostly frequented by students and young couples.

"I came forward when I saw Seena's face on the news," he said. "She was a regular. Used to come with a guy. Looked like her boyfriend."

"Did you know who he was at the time?" JD asked.

The café owner shook his head. "Not then. But later, in Dubai, I saw his face again on the news. His name's Kiran-caught in some financial scam."

"When was this?" JD pressed.

"Maybe six... eight months ago. I don't remember exactly."

Sarah leaned forward, eyes steady. "What else do you remember about them?"

"My place gets all kinds. I've seen fights, stolen kisses, and worse. As long as they pay, I don't care. That day, my staff was off, so I was on floor duty. I caught bits of their conversation. Seena seemed nervous. Kiran was calm-like he was explaining something."

"Explaining what?" Sarah asked.

"A case. I don't know the details. Seena kept saying she was scared. Kiran told her the case was closed, no one would come after her. He was reassuring-but she didn't look convinced."

Sarah noted it down. They collected what they could about Kiran and left, deciding to follow the lead.

Later that afternoon, Issac arrived at the same house. His visit was quiet. Unofficial.

The café owner repeated what he told Sarah and team. "Sir, I already told all this to some officers this morning. Am I in trouble?"

"No. They've asked me to follow up on some missed details," Issac said.

"I really did tell everything I know."

Issac gave a faint nod. "We're just tying loose ends. Did you ever see Seena or Kiran with anyone else? Before or after that day?"

The café owner paused, eyes narrowing as a memory surfaced. "Oh. I forgot to mention something."

Issac leaned in. "Go on."

"Right before they left, another man joined them. Then a couple. They pulled their chairs near my cashier counter. I overheard part of the conversation."

Issac opened his phone, flipping to photos of Ashok, Sandra, and Alfred. "Any of these familiar?"

The café owner studied them, then nodded. "That's them. "This guy" he pointed at Ashok "he came in first."

"What did you hear?"

"Seena was upset. She said someone had visited her at school. Sounded shaken. Asked about transferring back to her hometown."

"What did he say?"

"He said he could help. Said Mr. Williams was a friend and could arrange it."

Issac's tone sharpened. "Did she mention who visited her?"

"No, sir… but…" He hesitated. "But what?"

"I don't think those people were… normal." "What makes you say that?"

"When the other couple joined them (Sandra and Alfred) I got suspicious. Their body language, the way they talked… I think they were into partner swapping."

Issac stayed silent.

"I overheard Ashok say a girl from Dubai was in town. He was excited. Mentioned he was going to meet her. Kiran said he wanted to see her too."

"Hafsana?" Issac asked.

"Yes, something like that. Ashok said her landline was out, she called him from a cabbie's number. He told Kiran to wait a couple of days to reach out."

"Then what happened?"

"They split. Kiran left with the woman who came as couple. Seena left with the other guy. It all felt… off."

Issac stood. "Thank you."

The café owner walked him to the car, then hesitated. "Sir, can I ask you something?"

Issac opened the door, eyes unreadable. "Did any of them… kill that girl?"

Issac started the engine. "They're all dead."

Chapter 38
Find Him an find him fast

Sarah and her team had gathered intel on Kiran and summoned two of his former employees-his ex-manager and ex-accountant-to the interrogation room.

Both men claimed to have been with him from the start.

"Kiran had a gift," the accountant said. "Especially with numbers. The stock market was his playground. He made clients rich-and himself, even richer."

"Then you must know where he is now," Sarah said, sharp and to the point.

"Ma'am, I don't," the accountant replied. "The company didn't collapse-it was collapsed. It was deliberate."

Sarah said nothing, but her eyes shifted between them. The manager was twitchy, glancing at the floor between answers. The accountant was smooth-too smooth, rehearsed like someone used to covering financial fallout.

"By who?" she asked.

The accountant hesitated. "He had a weakness. Women. Every weekend, a different destination, a different woman. He lived big. Lavish parties. Fast cars. A lot of people didn't like that. Especially the old- rich crowd."

The manager nodded. "They got the media to say the company was sinking. Clients panicked. Wanted their money out."

Sarah folded her arms. "And the police arrested him."

"Yes," the accountant said. "I went to the station with him. But he didn't panic. He told the officers, 'Take me to the office.' When we got there, he stood in front of angry clients and promised the money would be in their accounts by evening."

"And was it?"

"Every rupee. With profit."

The manager added, "That's when we knew this wasn't about money. This was political."

The accountant continued. "His name got dragged. But he didn't flinch. Our office was on a ten-year lease. He called the landlord and said we'd be shutting down temporarily-but he wanted the space held. Gave us severance. Asked us to find other jobs."

"And then?" Sarah asked.

"Then he disappeared. No contact. Nothing."

"Friends? Social circle? Anyone who might know where he went?"

The manager shook his head. "He kept work and personal life separate. We never met his friends."

The accountant leaned in. "But I do have something-bank records. He'd occasionally transfer money to a few women. Labeled as 'consultation fees.' He had us enter it like that during tax filings."

"We'll need everything," Shanu said immediately.

"I have it all. On a hard disk. I can bring it tomorrow," the accountant replied.

"Photos?" Sarah asked.

"Some on my phone. More on my laptop. Office events. Clients, parties," the manager said.

After they left, Sarah stood by the window, still watching the hallway.

She didn't turn around when she spoke. "We have work to do."

The team straightened instinctively.

"Go through every photo. Every face. One of them knows where he is-or knows what he left behind."

Then, with her eyes still fixed ahead:

"Be ready. Tomorrow morning, we raid Kiran's office."

Chapter 39
Before the raid

Issac had already predicted Sarah's next move.

She'd go for Kiran's office-of course she would. But instead of waiting, Issac decided to get there first. He wasn't interested in red tape or procedure. He needed answers. And fast.

That night, under a cloudy sky and dead streetlights, Issac broke into the office.

It wasn't large-an older commercial space tucked away in a half-deserted business park. The perfect place for secrets to collect dust.

Inside, it was a mess. Chairs overturned, files scattered. He moved through the dark without a flashlight, relying on memory and moonlight. In the corner, behind a glass partition, he spotted a sleek office cabin. Probably Kiran's.

He broke in.

The air was stale. The place hadn't been touched in weeks. Everything screamed expensive-leather chair, polished desk, chrome fittings-but the dust dulled the shine.

He scanned quickly. The desktop still sat under the table, silent and untouched. No time to search it file by file. Issac dropped to his knees, unscrewed the CPU, and yanked out the hard disk.

As he stood, he noticed a card reader plugged into the machine-oddly placed. Kiran had probably used it for SD cards or mini storage.

The drawers were empty at first glance. Too empty. Issac pulled out the chair and sat down, closing his eyes for a second. Then he reached under the drawers-his fingers feeling for the uneven seam that didn't match the finish.

Click.

A false bottom slid free.

Inside was a small, sleek box-lined with velvet, fitted perfectly. He opened it to find several SD cards and a couple of pen drives, nestled like jewelry.

"Gotcha," he muttered, his voice low and dry.

The sky outside was beginning to soften, streaked with early light.

Time to go.

He pocketed everything, gave the place one last scan, and then slipped back out the way he came.

Sarah would be there in a few hours. But Issac had already been-and gone.

Chapter 40
Where Are You Hiding?

Sarah and her team arrived at Kiran's office just after sunrise. The landlord handed over the keys without much conversation. Before stepping inside, Sarah gave her instructions.

"Don't waste time on client lists. Look for anomalies. Files, drawers, digital backups-anything that looks out of place."

Inside, the dust made everything look undisturbed at first. But in Kiran's cabin, JD spotted the fractured edge of a glass panel.

"Something's off," he said. "That's not old damage."

Sarah stepped closer, examining the break. "Someone was here. Last night."

"You think it was Kiran?" Shanu asked. Sarah shook her head. "No."

"Why not?" VK asked.

Sarah's voice was steady. "He wouldn't need to break in. He'd have keys. He'd walk in and take what he needed."

The team exchanged uncertain glances. Shanu didn't look convinced. "Then who was it?"

Sarah didn't answer right away. She stared at the room like it had spoken to her in a language only she understood. Then, calmly:

"I think I know."

As they stepped outside toward the car, Shanu couldn't hold back. "What if Kiran's playing us? Making it look like someone else broke in to throw us off?"

JD nodded. "We haven't seen him in months. This could be a setup."

Sarah paused by the car. "Valid point," she said. Then, turning on her heel, "Let's go back in."

The team followed, curiosity ignited.

Back in Kiran's cabin, Sarah scanned the room again, this time with more intent. She walked to the attached restroom, opened the door, and paused.

A travel kit sat on the sink. She opened it-expensive cologne, a comb, unused condoms, and a few sachets of grooming creams.

She handed it to Shanu. "Send this for DNA testing. Now." As they turned to leave again, Sarah's eyes caught on something simple and obvious-a photo frame on the desk. Kiran's face, frozen in time. He looked confident. Too confident. Sarah stared at it for a moment, her expression unreadable. "He's handsome," she thought absently. Then, aloud-quiet, but edged with steel: "Where are you hiding?"

Chapter 41
Altitudes and Attitudes

The police bar wasn't just a watering hole-it was Issac's quiet
fortress. Dark wood interiors, soft classical music, and low
conversations among senior officers gave it a hush that suited him.
He liked his thoughts loud and the world quiet.

Sarah knew where to find him.

She walked in, scanning the room. He was in the far corner-alone,
scotch untouched, and face unreadable. Right where she expected.

She approached, straight-backed and uninvited.

"Hi. Sarah, CBI," she said, sliding onto the stool beside him. "Mind
if I join you?"

Issac didn't answer. But he didn't say no.

"I've taken over your case," she added, tone controlled, firm.

"So I heard." The words dropped like stones. No warmth, no
welcome.

Silence stretched. Sarah didn't flinch.

"What's your drink?" Issac finally asked, not looking at her.

"I'll have what you're having."

He motioned to the bartender. "Chivas 18 for her." Sarah raised an
eyebrow. "You've got good taste." "So do you," Issac said flatly.
"Apparently."

Her smile was small, testing. "Glad we agree on something."

Issac's eyes stayed forward.

Sarah shifted gears. "I wanted to ask you a few things about the case."

"I might not answer."

That line wasn't a threat. It was a boundary.

"I know how that feels," Sarah said, her voice softening. "You built the case. You did the groundwork. And now the Bureau steps in."

Issac didn't react.

"But I've studied your work," she continued. "You're exceptional. Unorthodox, maybe-but brilliant."

"Thanks," he said, in a tone that made it sound like anything but gratitude.

Her drink arrived. She took a sip, then leaned in.

"I'm not here to flatter you. I'm here to finish this case. And I'd like your help."

Issac finally turned. Met her eyes. Calm. Cold. "You assume I'm still on it."

"I don't assume," Sarah said. "I know." There it was-the flicker she was waiting for.

"Was it you last night?" she asked, keeping her voice level. "At Kiran's office?"

He gave a slow shake of the head. Nothing else.

"You could at least be bad at lying," she smirked. "I don't care if you're running your own side show. But if you've found something…"

"I told you," Issac said, voice low, measured. "Wasn't me."

Sarah leaned back, sizing him up.

"Who else would it be?" she said. "You like to win, Issac."

He didn't blink. "Is that what this is for you too?"

Sarah's patience cracked. "No. The goal is to catch the murderer. Close the damn case."

Issac leaned forward, just slightly. "Isn't that your job?" "It is. And I'll do it before you if you keep holding out."

The air between them felt electric-like something sharp was about to snap.

"I'm this close," she said, eyes locked on his. "Give me two days."

Issac raised his glass. "I'll drink to that."

Sarah tossed money on the bar and downed her scotch in one swift shot. "Then the drink's on me."

She walked out, not looking back.

Outside, the night was cool. Issac's car was parked where it always was. Sarah pulled a small black case from her bag, slipped out a GPS tracker, and knelt behind his rear plate.

Click.

Done.

No more shadows.

She rose, dusted her hands, and walked into the dark. Altitude met attitude!!

Chapter 42
Same Time, Same Night.

"VK, please tell me we've got something solid," Sarah said, her voice sharp with the residual burn of her encounter with Issac.

VK glanced up from his laptop, a faint grin tugging at his mouth. "I don't know if it's solid... but it's something."

Sarah sank into the couch, eyes locked on him. "Bring it on."

"Kiran's still in India-or was, until recently," VK began. "I cross-checked with immigration. No departure records under his name. I suspect he's either trying to get a new passport or already using a fake one."

Sarah sifted through Kiran's file on the table. "Passing biometric checks wouldn't be easy."

"Unless," VK countered, "he already had one." Sarah's eyes narrowed. "Yeah... that's possible."

"I also checked his bank activity. His cards are dormant. But the last ATM ping was in Calicut, near the railway station."

She leaned forward. "That's a long way from Cochin."

VK nodded. "And here's the kicker-he transferred around 20 million to foreign accounts before going dark."

Sarah blinked. "How the hell did he manage that?"

"Still figuring that out," VK admitted. "JD's chasing leads on the offshore trail. Once I get the full report, we might get a location."

"If we find him, we close this," Sarah muttered. "I want this done."

Just then, Shanu walked in, face unreadable, holding a folder with a red tag.

"I've got the DNA results," she said, handing it to Sarah.

Sarah took it, her hand instinctively steady-but something in Shanu's silence set her on edge. She flipped the file open.

A few lines. Two matches. Then the name.

Her breath caught. The room seemed to tilt for half a second.

Shanu spoke quietly, like dropping a stone in water. "The body at Viceroy House... it's Kiran's. DNA matched and confirmed."

VK stared at her, stunned. "No. That can't be."

Sarah looked up, her expression frozen-lips parted, eyes locked, but not seeing.

"He was supposed to be running," she murmured. "He was supposed to still be out there…"

Later, at the guesthouse dining table, JD joined them with a drink. VK and Shanu filled him in.

JD shook his head. "Six bodies now. Kiran's one of them. How many more are going to surface?"

Shanu, eyes locked on her files, barely acknowledged him.

"Have a drink, Shanu," VK teased. "Come on, take the edge off."

"I'll have one with Sarah," Shanu replied flatly, scribbling notes.

Moments later, Sarah walked in from the shower-hair damp, wearing shorts and a tee. She poured herself a drink, then poured another for Shanu.

She looked at the half-empty bottle.

"This is the last of what I brought," she said. "We better wrap this case before it runs dry."

Then, with a wry smile, "Also-I think Issac's still working the case. But I'm going to win this."

VK raised his glass. "Should we ask state police to back off?"

Sarah shook her head. "Let him play. I like challenges."

She handed Shanu her drink. "Besides, same goal-find the killer."

They raised their glasses-except Shanu, who suddenly froze.

"Whoa!" she gasped.

She grabbed two sheets from the file and shoved them at Sarah. "Look at this!"

Sarah scanned them quickly.

"Kiran's time of death… and Hafsana's. Same day. Almost the same hour."

Sarah's drink hit the table with a clink. "That's a connection."

"Anyone know where she lived?" she asked. "I do," JD said.

Sarah stood, already reaching for her keys. "Let's go." "Now?" VK groaned. "It's past midnight."

Sarah turned, her stare ice-cold.

She remembered what happened the last time she waited.

VK said nothing more.

The team grabbed their gear. They headed to Hafsana's house.

Chapter 43
This time, I am first

Hafsana's house stood in eerie isolation-an old structure set across from a vast, silent paddy field that stretched into the dark like a forgotten sea. Sparse homes dotted the landscape, making the soft neon glow from a lone streetlight near her gate the only point of reference. It cast just enough light to make the house visible-and unsettling.

As Sarah and her team pulled up, she muttered, "Who the hell chooses to live here?"

"It's haunted," Shanu said, stepping out. The endless trill of crickets and deep-throated croaks from the field wrapped around them like static.

"We'll need to break in," JD said, already heading to the car boot.

While JD and VK grabbed a few basic tools, Sarah walked the perimeter with her phone's flashlight. At the side of the house, she found the main switchboard-and something odd: a small key half-stuck behind the panel.

She flipped the porch light on, then pried the key loose.

"Try this," she said, handing it to JD. "Found it near the switchboard."

"Left for the cleaner, maybe?" Shanu guessed. The key turned with a satisfying click.

Inside, the air was stale but still held faint traces of perfume and cleaning agents. Two bedrooms and a hall. One bedroom door was slightly ajar. The other was sealed shut with a biometric lock.

All eyes turned to VK.

"Can you open it?"

"Not without my gear. It's back at the guest house."

"Then search what we can," Sarah said. She turned and exited the house.

Out on the road, Sarah scanned the surroundings. Just up ahead, a flickering fluorescent light revealed a tiny roadside shop-the only sign of life for miles. Two men stood outside, arguing. One was older, mid-sixties, slurring his words, clearly drunk. The other looked like the shopkeeper.

"I'm telling you, go sleep somewhere else," the shopkeeper snapped.

The old man wobbled in place. "This is public space," he barked back, then stumbled down, pulling out a ragged bedsheet from his sack. He was settling in under the shop awning.

As Sarah approached, his eyes caught the shape of her figure-and a smirk curled on his lips.

"Haven't seen you around here," he said, his voice oily, eyes sliding down to her shorts.

She ignored the tone. "Do you sleep here every night?"

He chuckled, misreading her completely. "You're American, huh? Figures. Yeah, yeah-this is my bedroom." He waved a hand around like royalty surveying his palace.

But as JD and VK emerged from the shadows behind her, his smirk vanished.

His eyes darted. Then widened.

Sarah gave a slight nod. JD and VK closed in.

The man's voice pitched into panic.

"Wait-who are you? Where are you taking me?!" No one answered.

He was done sleeping under the stars tonight.

Chapter 44
The Old Man and the 'See'

The old man was taken to the interrogation center and allowed to rest on the floor, half-drunk and exhausted. Sarah and her team returned briefly to the guest house to gather essentials, anticipating that he would be more cooperative once the alcohol wore off.

When they returned, they found him curled up, snoring peacefully on the cold floor. Sarah stared through the glass.

"How do we get him to talk?" she asked, more to herself than anyone. "He's too old to rough up."

JD stepped forward. "Let me try something. But I'll go in alone first, come in only when I signal"

He entered the room, eyes scanning for anything he could use. A steel tumbler sat on the edge of the table. JD lifted it and dropped it hard onto the floor.

The sharp clang shattered the silence.

The old man jolted upright, blinking against the fluorescent lights. "Where... where am I?"

JD ignored him and calmly began laying out a set of tools from his bag-nothing violent, just sharp and metallic. But it was enough.

The old man's eyes widened as his drunken mind filled in the blanks.

JD called out to no one in particular, "Can you pass me the pliers?"

That did it.

"Sir! Sir, wait! I'll speak!" the old man shouted, scrambling to his feet. "Please, I'll tell you!"

The moment the words left his mouth JD signaled Sarah and the door swung open.

Sarah stepped in first, followed by Shanu and VK. She crossed her arms, watching the old man with that signature stare that made even sober men squirm.

JD stayed leaned against the wall, arms folded. "Well done," Sarah said without looking at him.

JD gave the slightest shrug, but the faint grin on his face said enough.

Shanu smirked. "That was wicked."

VK chuckled. "Didn't know you were that creative under pressure."

"Comes with being underestimated," JD muttered, still keeping his eyes on the old man.

Sarah stepped closer. "Alright, old man. You wanted to talk. Start."

He didn't need convincing anymore.

"I sleep outside the shop, sir. Every night. That day-it was the church carnival. Noise everywhere. I got to my usual spot around 2 AM."

He took a deep breath.

"I was facing the girl's house. That's when I saw someone jump over her wall. Landed clean. There was a bike waiting on the road. He got on and took off-fast. Came right past me. I pretended to sleep, but I got a good look."

"And?" JD asked.

"It was Giri. A small-time thief. I've seen him around. Couple days later, when the news broke that the girl had gone missing, I went to ask him about it."

"You confronted him?" JD raised an eyebrow.

The old man nodded. "He didn't say much. Just gave me some cash and told me to keep quiet. Said the girl wasn't even there."

"Where does he stay?" Sarah asked. "Pandit Colony," the old man replied.

Shanu looked up sharply. "That's near Viceroy House." The team exchanged glances.

"We'll let you go once we find Giri," JD said flatly. Sarah gave a nod.

"Let's move," she said.

As they left the room, VK muttered under his breath, "I just hope he's still alive."

He didn't need to explain why-every lead they'd chased so far had ended up dead.

Chapter 45

Too Late

While Sarah and her team set off toward Pandit Colony to chase down Giri, Issac made his own move-heading for Hafsana's house. But he didn't go straight in.

Instead, he parked his bike at the lone shop that sat like a sentinel at the edge of the road, the only flicker of life in the rural silence. He dismounted slowly, eyes scanning the area, then stepped toward the shuttered counter.

The shopkeeper noticed him and stood up with a start. He didn't need a badge to know Issac was a cop-he'd seen enough in his lifetime to spot one in plain clothes.

"You the owner?" Issac asked, voice low and steady.

"Yes, sir," the man replied, his tone respectful. "We sell fertilizers. Not much else."

"What time do you usually close?"

"No fixed time, sir. Depends on who shows up. Business is slow here."

Issac leaned in slightly. "What about on church carnival day?"

The man hesitated, trying to remember. "That day? We don't open at all. I go for Mass in the morning... and no one really buys anything. Everyone's either at the church or drunk off their heads by noon."

Issac's eyes wandered to the corner near the side wall. A bundle of rags, old cigarette butts, and a flattened pillow of newspapers lay in a forgotten heap.

"Those?" he asked.

The shopkeeper nodded quickly. "An old man used to sleep there. Regular. Never missed a night." Issac stepped closer, examining the scene. "Where is he now?"

The shopkeeper scratched his head. "No idea, sir. First time I've seen his things just lying there like that. He's usually gone by the time I open, but he never leaves his rags behind. I was wondering myself…"

But Issac wasn't.

He straightened up, jaw tightening. He was too late.

Sarah had already been here.

Chapter 46
Behind the Cupboard

The streets of Pandit Colony still wore the hush of early morning. Lights flickered awake in a few houses, but the lanes were mostly empty, save for the low hum of ceiling fans and the first cries of crows.

Sarah and her team were already in position, stationed like silent sentries around a modest, dilapidated house tucked into a narrow alley. JD had done the initial recon-no lights inside, doors bolted. Giri wasn't home.

"Either he's crashed elsewhere or he's on his way," JD murmured, eyes fixed down the lane.

A few minutes later, their patience paid off.

Giri came strolling up the street, slow and relaxed, his gait that of a man used to blending into shadows. Maybe he'd just returned from a job. Maybe he thought the world was still sleeping.

But when he spotted JD lingering at the corner-too tall, too clean, and too watchful-his body stiffened.

Wrong place. Wrong face.

In an instant, Giri spun on his heel and bolted, his instincts kicking in like a switchblade.

But he didn't run far.

Sarah had chosen her spot well-half in shadow, half in wait. Giri charged blindly, looking over his shoulder.

He never saw the leg sweep coming.

Her boot hit just below his knee. Giri flipped forward and slammed into the dirt, the wind knocked out of him before he could scream. JD and VK pounced.

Within seconds, he was cuffed, dragged back into his own house, and shoved into a chair.

The house smelled like stale food, sweat, and something sour-fear maybe.

"Talk," JD said, standing over him. Giri spat to the side. "I didn't kill her."

"No one said you did, "Sarah replied, her voice razor-thin. "Start from the beginning."

At first, he played dumb. Then JD backhanded him across the face-just enough to ring the bell without cracking the glass.

"I'll talk," Giri coughed. "It was the church carnival night."

He licked his lips.

"I saw the Uber drop her off in the afternoon. I figured she was alone-as usual. Always is. Stays for a few days then disappears again. Everyone else is either at church or drunk on that day. Seemed like the perfect window."

He looked down at the floor, like the details were tied to the cracks in the tiles.

"I showed up around three in the morning. No sound inside. The AC wasn't running. That's usually a good sign that nobody's home."

"The front door wasn't even locked," he added. "I slipped in, tried the first room-no luck. Some fancy lock. So I hit the second one."

He sniffed, then continued.

"Wardrobe was open. Gold and cash. Jackpot. On the way out, I saw a laptop bag on the dining chair. Looked expensive."

"So you took it?" VK asked.

"Yeah. Then locked the door behind me and bailed."

Sarah narrowed her eyes. "And when you heard she was dead?"

"I panicked. Took the gold to Chennai-split it, sold it in different shops. Thought about dumping the laptop but…"

"But?" JD growled.

Giri gestured toward the kitchen. "It's still here. Behind the cupboard."

JD hauled him to his feet and shoved him forward. "Show me."

Giri stumbled into the kitchen, climbed up, and reached behind the stained wooden cupboard. He pulled out a dusty black bag and handed it over.

Sarah opened it. Sleek. Clean. Untouched. "You didn't try to sell it?" she asked, skeptical.

"I knew they'd trace it," Giri said. "Didn't want that heat."

JD gave a dark laugh. "Smart thief."

Sarah nodded toward the door. "Let's get him to the interrogation center. We'll see how smart he is once we crack that laptop."

Chapter 47
Into the cloud

Back at headquarters, VK hunched over the iMac pulled from Giri's kitchen. His fingers were working a rhythm-sharp, fast, deliberate. The rest of the team buzzed around him.

Inside the laptop bag, they'd found an Android phone-its screen cracked but still functional. After a quick sweep, they confirmed it belonged to Kiran.

But that only deepened the mystery.

How had Kiran's phone and laptop ended up at Hafsana's house? If both Kiran and Hafsana were murdered together why were their bodies found in separate places? And more importantly-who moved them? Who killed them? Why?

Sarah, meanwhile, was handling the political side. She met with the Joint Director, briefing him on the arrests of the old man and Giri. She clarified they weren't suspects in the killings but emphasized they should remain in custody-for now.

Privately, she just didn't want Issac getting to them first.

Back at the guest house, JD and Shanu were deep in phone call logs from Kiran's Android. Mostly dead ends. Office contacts. Sanitized communication.

"Any updates?" Sarah asked, walking in.

"Phone's clean," Shanu replied. "It's a burner. Strictly work. I sent some numbers to cyber cell, but I'm not holding my breath."

"Gallery?" Sarah asked.

"Office functions. Spreadsheets. Maybe a blurry picture

Of a sandwich," JD muttered. "Useless."

"We already have those from Kiran's colleagues," Shanu added.

Just then, VK leaned back from the desk, grinning. "I'm in."

Kiran's picture filled the iMac screen. The team crowded around.

Their smiles faded fast.

No browser history. No files. Just duplicates of what was already on the Android.

"This is disappointing," JD said, frowning.

"Not yet," Sarah replied, her voice low and focused. "We all agree-Kiran's a fraudster?"

They nodded.

"Fraudsters use second phones. Right?" More nods.

"What kind?" Sarah asked. "IPhone. For sure," VK answered. "Why?"

"Privacy. Security."

Sarah stepped closer. "And where do iPhones store data?"

VK lit up. "ICloud."

"And that's linked to…?" she prompted.

"His Apple ID. If the iMac was his main machine, the cloud's probably linked to it."

VK typed fast, eyes sharp. A window popped up-iCloud login. Password protected.

JD leaned in. "Can you crack it?"

VK's smirk was pure mischief. "I can crack anything under the sun."

The room went quiet. Shanu stood. JD paced. Sarah folded her arms and stared at the screen.

Minutes ticked.

Then VK leaned back, slow and smug. "And I did it again."

A soft chime echoed through the room. The iCloud opened.

The team gathered close, eyes locked on the screen. Inside the cloud-Kiran's secrets waited.

Chapter 48
Unearthed

Issac drove down the winding road, the trees casting long shadows in the fading light. The clock read 5 PM, but the dense foliage made it feel like night, forcing him to switch on the headlights. The Viceroy's house loomed ahead, its colonial grandeur now shrouded in decay. The artificial lake nearby seemed to whisper secrets, its glassy surface reflecting the skeletal branches above. Ever since Kiran's body was found here, the government had suspended demolition plans, leaving the place to rot in silence-a haunted monument to unresolved death.

He stepped out of the car and scanned the area. Crickets and frogs echoed in the stillness. The entrance was sealed with police tape-*Do Not Enter. Crime Scene.* Issac pulled a glove from his pocket and slipped it on. He ducked under the tape and moved through the ruined corridors, making his way toward the back-toward the lake.

The waterline had receded in the summer heat, revealing a patch of cracked earth and scattered stones. Issac walked the edge, his gaze sharp, searching. When the twig he was using struck something hard, he dropped to his knees and began to dig with frantic urgency. His fingers uncovered the corner of a phone-an iPhone, weathered but intact.

But before he could examine it, instinct screamed too late.

A heavy object slammed into the side of his head. White pain exploded in his skull. The world tilted violently as he crashed to the ground. His vision dimmed, blurred. Blood pooled in his right eye. And as the black closed in, he saw a dark figure approaching-blurred, silent, final.

When Issac came to consciousness, he was slumped against a wall. His head throbbed from the impact, and the warm trickle of blood down his temple reminded him he was still alive-barely. The setting sun poured through the fractured glass, turning dust into gold.

Then, a voice, smooth and distant. "I told you I'd win this case."

Sarah stood framed in the sun, the iPhone he'd just unearthed now in her hands.

The same phone that had been uploaded to iCloud. The same phone VK had broken into.

But how had Issac known where it was buried?

Chapter 49
Play It Again

After Ashok, Sandra, and Alfred's deaths-and Seena's disappearance-Kiran grew restless. He traveled quietly, taking a train to avoid notice, and arrived in Cochin under a false name. He had only one real reason to return: Hafsana.

She wasn't just a lover. She was his most trusted link in a havala network, laundering money into offshore accounts. That day, he brought a bag full of cash-meant for an urgent transfer to Australia, where he hoped to vanish into a new identity. But the bag would never reach its destination. It ended up with Giri.

Their meeting took place during the evening of the church carnival. Inside Hafsana's biometric-secured room, the door had been left slightly open. It was a quiet oversight-practical, unthinking, maybe to let in air-but it made everything that followed possible.

They lay in bed, the atmosphere muted. The killings had come too close. Seena was missing. Hafsana, usually composed, admitted she was afraid.

Kiran stroked her hand and said softly, *"We won't see each other again for a while. Let's take a picture."*

He picked up his iPhone and opened it. The camera app had last been used in video mode. As soon as the screen unlocked, it defaulted back-recording automatically.

Kiran, unaware, tried to flip from the front to the rear camera. His thumb hovered over the switch icon.

Then the door creaked.

His gaze shifted-confused, not yet alarmed. "Wait-who-"

The hammer came down. Once.

Twice.

Kiran collapsed, the phone slipping from his hands. It hit the floor with a soft thud-lens-up, recording the ceiling at a tilted angle.

Hafsana screamed. She scrambled off the bed, barefoot and panicked. But the man-Issac-was already moving.

One blow silenced her. Another made it final. Then silence.

Issac stood over them, breathing hard. He wiped the hammer clean with clinical precision, then bent down and picked up the phone.

He didn't check it. He didn't unlock it.

He simply slipped it into his pocket and walked out-unaware the video had just started recording... and was already syncing to iCloud.

Later that night, he wrapped the bodies separately. Kiran was buried behind the Viceroy's house. Hafsana was left in an abandoned, disputed property near the backwaters-her grave hidden among weeds and salt-warped debris.

The room was wiped clean, closed up like nothing had ever happened.

Issac thought it was over.

But the phone had remembered.

And now-years later-it was ready to play again.

Chapter 50
Seven not six!!

"A very successful police officer. In our group sessions at the CBI, we used to study your cases," Sarah said, holding up the nearly rusted iPhone. Her voice was steady, but her eyes were cold. "We admired your brilliance, Issac. But this one silly mistake..."

Issac lunged, reaching for the phone. Sarah was faster.

They collided with brutal force. The fight exploded into motion-sharp, instinctive, desperate. Sarah had combat training, honed through covert ops with RAW. But Issac wasn't fighting to hurt her. He wasn't here to kill. He just wanted one thing:

"The evidence".

Their hands locked. Elbows cracked against ribs. Shoulders slammed into the peeling wall, sending up a cloud of dust. Grunts and gasps echoed through the hollow house.

Sarah struck with a clean, low kick-controlled, surgical. Issac staggered back, clutching his side. She moved in to press the advantage, but his raw strength surged again. They clashed-two forces unraveling.

Finally, both collapsed to the ground-bruised, breathless, and bleeding at the knuckles.

"I've made copies," Sarah said, still gasping. She cradled her ribs but never let go of the phone. "Destroying this one won't save you."

Her eyes narrowed-fury and disbelief swirling behind them.

"This is unbelievable. A great officer-committing six murders? For what? For nothing?"

Her voice cracked, disbelief tipping into rage.

Issac's head hung low. His chest heaved. Then he looked up-eyes sharp, jaw clenched.

"Wrong," he said. "It's not six. It's seven." A long silence. Sarah froze.

"There are seven of them," he continued, his voice calm now. Dead calm. "And there's a reason."

The words settled like lead.

Sarah's control snapped. "What? Who else, Issac?" she barked. Her voice was raw, caught between fury and panic. "What possible reason could justify this? What the hell happened to you?"

He didn't flinch. He didn't blink.

But in his silence, something cracked open. And it wasn't just between them.

Chapter 51
She Was My Heart

"Do you have a girl child?" Issac asked abruptly.

Sarah, still catching her breath, hesitated-then nodded.

Issac stared ahead, as if looking through the cracked wall and into a life long buried.

"I had one too," he said. "Aaliya. That was her name. Blue eyes. Always smiling. I adopted her from the same orphanage I grew up in."

His voice softened, breaking at the edges. "She became my life. And I was hers."

He paused. Sarah said nothing. Something about his tone-raw, unfinished-told her this wasn't the moment to speak. She let the silence breathe.

"But my wife... Ineya..." he muttered, and then stopped. A shadow crossed his face. He clenched his jaw, trying to suppress something that had no name.

"Do you know what adoption really is?" he asked suddenly, eyes fixed on her.

Sarah remained quiet, the tension still fresh from their fight, both of them bruised, both of them sitting on the cold floor like fractured remnants.

"When someone is born... from the heart," Issac whispered.

His voice cracked. "She was my heart."

Tears welled up in one eye. Sarah couldn't tell if it was sorrow or rage-or both.

"She fell," he said quietly. "From the top of her school building. Head injury. Died on the spot."

He blinked slowly, as if trying to process it again.

"I went to collect her things a few days later..." His words drifted off, swallowed by the weight of memory.

Silence followed.

It wasn't just sadness. It was something else. Something about to erupt.

And Sarah could feel it.

The seventh name was close. And the story wasn't over.

Chapter 52
They're All Dead

The school's staff room was on the fifth floor-the same floor as Aaliya's classroom.

Issac stepped in, his legs heavy, his mind fogged with grief. Seena, Aaliya's class teacher, stood near a desk with a cardboard box in her hands. She greeted him with a practiced solemnity.

"Sir, please come and take a seat. I'm really sorry for your loss," she said softly. "We're still trying to process it ourselves."

Issac sat slowly, the ache in his chest worsening.

Seena placed the box on the table and gently handed him a composition book. Its cover was worn, its pages filled with Aaliya's neat handwriting.

Issac opened it.

My father, my hero.

The words stopped his breath. In the corner, she had drawn a small Star of David-the pendant he had given her. She wore it every day. He hadn't seen her without it.

The ache became unbearable. Then came a knock.

A schoolgirl stood at the doorway, her eyes darting between Seena and Issac. "Ma'am, may I come in?" she asked.

Seena's expression changed instantly. Her voice sharpened. "What do you want?"

"My teacher asked me to collect the composition books," the girl said, barely audible.

"Then get it and go," Seena snapped, her irritation stark and out of place.

Issac lifted his head. He had felt it-the shift. The sudden tension in Seena's posture, the way she gripped the table tighter. It didn't match her earlier tone. And the girl… she kept glancing at him like she wanted to speak but couldn't.

She gathered the books quickly, her movements stiff. As she passed Issac, their eyes met.

Something unspoken passed between them. A flicker of fear. A buried truth.

Issac rose. "Thank you, Miss," he said quietly.

Seena gave a polite nod, but her eyes didn't meet his.

Out in the corridor, the air felt heavier. Issac walked toward the stairs.

"Uncle… Uncle," a small voice called behind him. He turned.

The same girl stood there, tense, clutching her books to her chest. She kept checking over her shoulder toward the staff room.

Issac bent down, his tone gentle. "What is it?"

"Aaliya was my best friend," she whispered. "The day she died… she came to class only in the afternoon. Her mom was there, so nobody asked anything. And I saw another uncle in the car…"

Her voice faded, but her eyes didn't. Then she leaned in closer, trembling. "Uncle… Seena teacher is bad."

And before he could ask more, she turned and ran down the corridor, disappearing into her class.

Issac's hands curled into fists.

He walked back to the staff room quietly.

Seena was on the phone. She stood with her back to the door, unaware he was behind her.

"Kiran… I was really, really scared," she was saying, her voice low, urgent. "Please be careful next time, please."

Issac froze.

"No, no, he didn't have any doubt," she continued quickly. "We *all* need to meet in the evening. I'll come to the café. Let's not contact each other again till it cools down."

She listened to what he had to say.

"You can say that, but I don't want to go to jail," she said with a firm edge. "Okay. Evening it is."

She sighed.

Then paused.

A flicker of something passed through her spine-she sensed it.

She spun around.

But Issac was already gone. Slipped out like a ghost.

Chapter 53
Behind the Glass

Issac's driver helped him place the box from the school into the back seat. As he opened the car door, something caught his eye in the reflection of the window.

Seena.

She was watching him from the fifth-floor corridor, face unreadable, arms crossed over her chest.

He got in without reacting. The engine hummed to life.

Inside the car, Issac pulled out his phone and dialed the number saved as "Love." Ineya didn't answer.

He tried again. Nothing.

Then he dialed another number.

"George, its Issac. I'm going to send you a number. I need it traced. Urgently."

He ended the call, his mind already spiraling. Moments later, the phone rang back.

"Sir… this number belongs to your wife?" George asked.

"Yes," Issac replied, his voice clipped. "She's not picking up. I need to find her. Now."

There was a pause. Then George responded, "Her phone's pinging near the old passport office tower. Close to Passport Road."

"Got it. Thanks, George." Issac hung up and told his driver, "Old Passport Road. Now."

Minutes later, he spotted Ineya's car parked near a strip of high-end restaurants. His eyes narrowed. She always picked the poshest place wherever she went. And there it was-her car outside a boutique café that had just opened for the day.

Issac walked up to the glass door. And froze.

Through the clear glass, he saw them. Ineya.

And Kiran.

Sitting together. Close. Laughing.

He didn't enter. Not yet. He stood there, just beyond the reach of sound, watching.

She didn't see him.

She looked at her smartwatch-his name flashing on the screen.

She declined the call.

Issac stepped inside silently and took a seat behind them, back straight, breath shallow. They hadn't noticed.

Kiran's hand was resting on her thigh.

"I'm tired of being here, Kiran," Ineya said, her voice low. "I don't think Issac and I can keep this going. I have a friend in Delhi. I might move there soon."

"Friend? He or she?" Kiran asked, half-smiling.

"Oh my god, you're a jealous pig," she said, laughing. "Of course I will be, you're the best." Kiran said "Lay?" she said, teasing.

"You say the same thing to Seena. And Sandra," she smirked.

"Who's jealous now?" Kiran countered.

Issac felt something tighten inside him. Not jealousy. Not betrayal.

Just cold.

Stillness.

Kiran's voice returned, softer now. "By the way, Seena called earlier. Your husband went to see her."

"For what?" Ineya asked, suddenly more alert. "Nothing major. He went to collect Aaliya's stuff." "Oh," she said, shrugging. "Okay."

That was it. Issac stood. No drama.

No confrontation.

He walked out, unnoticed.

Back through the same glass door he had entered.

Chapter 54
That's Why

Issac sat in the darkened living room, cradling a half-empty glass. The silence in the house pressed down on him like a weight. Outside, he heard the crunch of gravel-her car.

Ineya walked in, her heels clicking on the tile. She didn't look at him.

"Don't move," Issac said quietly. His voice carried something new-something final.

She paused at the doorway, arms folded. But her posture was casual. Dismissive.

"Where were you?" he asked, barely able to keep the tremor out of his voice.

She smirked. "Well… who wants to know?"

The glass flew from his hand and exploded against the floor.

"Your husband," he snarled.

She turned then-smiling like he was pathetic.

"You *were* Issac. Not anymore," she said. "We've been strangers for years. When's the last time you touched me? Or even saw me? You were always married to your goddamn job."

He didn't reply. He just stared.

His eyes drifted toward the parapet. The violin. Aaliya's violin. Untouched. Waiting.

"I need to ask you something," he said, each word shaking as it left him. "You dropped Aaliya to school that afternoon. Where were you… "

Ineya didn't let him finish.

"That bitch is dead," she snapped. "Why the f*** are you still-"

The violin cracked across her face before she could finish.

She dropped instantly, her head slamming against the floor, blood beginning to spread beneath her temple.

Issac stood over her, shaking. A guttural breath tore from his chest.

And then he saw her phone.

He knelt, picked it up. It's locked.

He grabbed her wrist. Pressed her thumb to the sensor. It clicked open.

The gallery launched.

Selfies. Dozens. Filters, pouts. Some barely dressed. He kept scrolling.

Then-Aaliya.

Photos of her. In shorts. Candid. Vulnerable. Some taken without her knowing. One in the bathroom, half-clothed.

His breathing turned shallow. Then came the video.

Aaliya sat stiffly on a couch in an unfamiliar room. Kiran was beside her, smiling too wide.

"I think she's shy," Ineya's voice said off-camera-cheerful. Playful.

"Isn't uncle handsome?" Kiran asked, inching closer. Aaliya's lips moved. But no sound came. Her eyes begged. Her hands clutched the edge of the couch.

"Let's go. Please." Her hands signed the words, desperate and trembling.

Issac froze.

"I'll be in the next room," Ineya said. The video cut out.

Issac blinked. Once. Then again.

As if staring longer would erase what he'd seen. The phone buzzed.

A WhatsApp message from Kiran. Issac opened it.

A photo of Aaliya's best friend-her classmate. The same girl who had warned him in the corridor.

"Isn't she cute?" kirans message Read. Another message followed.

"Seena said she'll help. Now don't get jealous." Issac's pulse became thunder in his ears.

The walls seemed to shrink. He turned to Ineya.

She was groaning. Coming to. He didn't think.

He didn't feel.

He reached for the nearest thing-a flower vase-and brought it down on her head.

Once.

Twice.

The third strike shattered her skull. Blood sprayed the wall. Her limbs twitched once, then fell still.

Issac stood over her, chest rising and falling like a storm.

He bent down again. Used her thumb. Reopened the phone.

He opened the chat. Typed slowly:

"Cut contacts. Husband suspicious" He sent it.

Then rose. Silent. Hollow.

He walked to the storage room. Picked up a hammer.

Then a pickaxe.

The floor was cold concrete. It screamed with each blow, but he didn't stop.

Hour after hour, he dug-through the stone, the dust, the bone-deep silence.

By dawn, Ineya was gone.

Her body buried beneath the place she once drank her coffee and scrolled through the lives she helped ruin.

Issac rebuilt it.

Tile. Mortar. Paint. Quiet.

Then he placed a Bible on the new ledge, opened to a bookmarked page.

Proverbs 31:8-9

"Speak up for those who cannot speak for themselves, for the rights of all who are destitute.

Speak up and judge fairly; defend the rights of the poor and needy." He sat beside it. Not praying. Just breathing.

And

"That's why "

Chapter 55
The Last Shot

By the time Issac finished his story, Sarah's team burst into the scene.

What they walked into stopped them cold.

Issac and Sarah-both drenched in blood. Clothes torn. Faces bruised. Neither speaking. Just breathing.

JD rushed to Sarah's side, panic in his voice. "Sarah, are you okay?"

She gave a slow, blood-smeared thumbs-up.

Then she turned toward VK. Her voice was hoarse, but steady. "Help him up," she said, motioning to Issac.

"But touch him with respect."

VK hesitated for a moment, then stepped forward and gently helped Issac to his feet. The rest of the team exchanged confused, unsettled glances.

"Long story," Sarah muttered. "Let's go. I need the last shot of my whiskey."

They loaded into the car, silence hanging like mist. Shanu handed Sarah a few wet tissues. She wiped her face clean and passed the rest to Issac.

Turning slightly, she glanced back. "VK?"

"Yes, Sarah?" he replied, still trying to make sense of the scene.

"You're the best ethical hacker I've ever worked with." VK blinked. "Thank you. That means a lot."

Before he could say more, Sarah lifted a finger. "Shh." JD pulled the car over beneath a streetlight. The road was quiet. Pale   yellow light spilled across the windshield.

VK leaned forward. "What do you need me to do, Sarah?"

Sarah didn't turn around.

"I want you to erase that evidence," she said softly. "Forever."

The silence returned. This time, heavier.

Somewhere in the distance, a dog barked. The city began to stir.

And the car moved and in the car no one asked a single question.

"Justice, this time, was personal."

Dedication

For Aaliya,

Who couldn't scream, but still begged for help.

 And for every child this world failed to protect. Your silence won't be forgotten.

This was always your story.

A Note beyond the Story
This wasn't just fiction. It's a mirror.

India registers over *1.5 lakh cases under the POCSO Act (Protection of Children from Sexual Offences)* every year. But the real number is much higher. Most cases never see a courtroom. Some never leave the home. And many victims grow up believing what happened to them was either their fault-or something to be buried forever.

Why?

Because we don't listen.

Too many parents dismiss their child's early warnings. A cry about someone "touching strangely" is brushed off as childish fantasy. Teachers and guardians look the other way. Families choose reputation over protection. The result?

The child carries that silence. And that silence grows. Inappropriate touch during early childhood leaves scars far beyond physical. Many teens who struggle with gender confusion or fractured identities later in life have one thing in common-they were 'molested or abused' as children.

Ask them. You'll hear stories that should have been stopped when they were five… six… eight years old. But we didn't listen. We didn't believe. We were too uncomfortable to talk. Or too busy to act. It's time we change. Start at home. Teach children what is appropriate and inappropriate touch. Use clear language. Don't leave it to cartoons or schools. Let them know they will never be punished for speaking out. Create space for trust, not shame.

If a child comes to you-listen first, protect second, act immediately. There are no second chances when it comes to abuse. One ignored sign can shape a lifetime.

To the law-makers, the justice system, and every adult reading this-**punishment must match the trauma**. Some crimes do not deserve leniency. And maybe it's time we ask if certain crimes-especially against children-deserve *capital punishment*.

"It would be better for them to be thrown into the sea with a millstone tied around their neck than to cause one of these little ones to stumble. -Luke 17:2

This story ends here.

But for thousands of children, the story is still unfolding.

Make sure you're not the one who stayed silent when they needed help the most.

Be the one who listens. Be the one who acts. Be Issac-before it's too late.

-Shyam